MAGIC & MARRIAGE

STARRY HOLLOW WITCHES, BOOK 15

ANNABEL CHASE

RED PALM PRESS LLC

Copyright © 2021 by Annabel Chase

All rights reserved.

No part of this book may be reproduced in any form or by any electronic or mechanical means, including information storage and retrieval systems, without written permission from the author, except for the use of brief quotations in a book review.

❀ Created with Vellum

PROLOGUE

"You know the rules," my father said. "First one to finish the task wins." He wore his trademark blue jacket, white shirt, and a dark blue ascot adorned with tiny white stars. There were fifty visible stars on the ascot. I knew because I'd counted them many times over the years, usually during one of his lectures on decorum or upholding the family legacy.

"What's the prize today, Father?" I asked. I was eagerness personified.

He stared down his patrician nose at me. "Albert has prepared a phenomenal chocolate mousse for dessert this evening."

I gasped. "That's my favorite."

He smiled proudly, as though I'd unearthed a secret. "So it is."

"And mine," my younger brother said.

My father held up a finger. "Ah, but there is only one and mousse cannot be split in half, so don't even think about invoking the wisdom of Solomon."

Although I disagreed with his assessment—in my

opinion mousse could be divided any which way—I kept silent. My brother glanced at me with his usual hangdog expression. I averted my gaze and strengthened my resolve to win. Nathaniel's pathetic face was a tactic to garner sympathy from me and nothing more. He wanted to win every bit as much as I did. How could he not? He was a Rose, after all. A descendant of the One True Witch. We were born with power other witches and wizards could only dream of. If our father tasked us with flying to the moon, we'd polish our broomsticks and find a way to make it happen or we'd die trying.

My mother waltzed into the room, taking a long, deep drag of her clove cigarette. "Do you not think it's a bit cruel, darling? You know how much they both adore the mousse."

My father turned to look at her. "Precisely why it's a worthy prize. What would be the point in having them compete over rice pudding? Neither one of them likes it enough to put in the effort."

"I suppose you have a point." My mother sank onto the settee with the grace of an open parachute kissing the ground. I'd defy anyone to find a more elegant woman in all of Starry Hollow.

My father motioned to our wands that hung on the wall like celebrated artwork. "Go on then. Let's get started. I have a cricket match in an hour. I'd like you to impress me well before then so I have something to boast about aside from my athletic prowess."

My mother's laughter tinkled like the dainty silver bell she used to summon the staff. "Oh, darling. You're simply too much."

I shot past my brother and was the first to retrieve my wand. A good start.

I wanted the chocolate mousse, of course, but even more

than that, I wanted the approval of my parents. It was an endless cycle. I'd manage to curry their favor one day, only to lose it the next. Their adoration was fickle and fleeting, therefore, it was up to me to secure it over and over again.

Despite my brother's younger age, he was talented, which made him a worthy opponent. My father said that we had only each other as competitors because no one else's powers came close. That meant no one else was in a position to challenge us and help us improve. I must've looked sad because my mother then offered a reassuring smile and reminded me it was lonely at the top. *The sooner you accept it, the happier you'll be.* Her words did little to raise my spirits. I didn't want to be lonely. I wanted to be like Autumn Basil-Wood with her endless party invitations and engaging smile. Everybody at the Black Cloak Academy adored her, students and teachers alike. She wasn't intimidating in the least.

But only because she was weak. More than once Father commented that her magic must've been diluted by interspecies breeding somewhere in her history because a Basil-Wood combination should've resulted in more impressive offspring. I hated when he spoke of children like livestock. I was no more a prized unicorn than Autumn was.

"What's the challenge, Father?" I asked.

"The first one to complete the puzzle using only magic wins." He stepped aside to reveal two sets of three-dozen enormous pieces on the floor. One for each of us.

I knew from experience this wasn't a typical puzzle. First we'd need to use reveal magic to show the imagery. Then we'd need to use magic to rotate the pieces. Then more magic to place the pieces in their proper position, which sometimes took several attempts before getting it right. Movement magic was harder than it looked.

"Ready, steady, go!" my father's voice rang out. He joined my mother on the settee to observe us. He never missed a beat. If I hesitated, he'd chastise me. If I made a wrong move, he'd criticize it. If there'd been a referee involved, my father would've been tossed out of the stands.

I had magic puzzles down to a science. First I revealed all the pieces to see the image in its entirety. This puzzle was an image of Thornhold. Under less pressurized circumstances, I'd think it was fun to solve a puzzle of our family home.

But nothing that happened at Thornhold could be described as fun.

I felt the intensity of my parents' gaze as they watched us perform. We were poodles jumping through hoops for their amusement. Once we'd finished, my parents would move on to another form of entertainment. Father would attend his cricket match and Mother would listen to music. They were, if nothing else, predictable.

Out of the corner of my eye, I noticed my brother had fallen behind. I only needed to maneuver three more pieces, whereas he needed five. Nathaniel must've had the same realization because he looked at me with tears shining in his eyes.

Oh, no. No tears. Do. Not. Cry.

The tears weren't an effort to manipulate me. They were genuine and I willed them away. At the mere hint of tears, my father would make Nathaniel start over. It was an unwritten rule. *There's no crying in magic*, he'd say, *unless children's tears are one of the ingredients*. Which they sometimes were.

Only one piece left to go. I cast a sidelong glance at my brother to see him struggling with the third-to-last piece.

Between the awkward shape of the piece and its position, it had been tricky.

A single tear slid down his cheek and I felt a twinge of sympathy. It started in my stomach and quickly spread to my extremities, gnawing at my bones with greedy little teeth. I did the only thing I could think of.

I dropped my wand.

"Clumsy oaf," I scolded myself. I reached down to scoop up the wand as Nathaniel locked the final piece of the puzzle into place.

My parents clapped. "Well done, Nathaniel," my father said.

My brother managed to wipe away the stray tear before my parents noticed it. "Thank you, Father."

My father clucked his tongue at me. "That was simply dreadful, Hyacinth. You should've won that quite easily."

My gaze dropped to the floor. I knew every crack in the wood. Every hairline fracture. I didn't dare calculate how many cumulative hours I'd spent staring at the floor in defeat and humiliation. Too many.

"I'm sorry, Father. I tried my best." My voice was barely audible.

"If that's your best, then I'm even more disappointed. Are you or are you not a Rose, Hyacinth?"

I lifted my chin and met his formidable gaze. "I am a Rose, Father. Through and through."

"Good, then chin up and start acting like one. You don't want to embarrass yourself by being mediocre when you're capable of so much more."

As predicted, my father left for his match and my mother lost herself in music in the parlor room. My brother and I ate our respective meals in silence. Our parents rarely joined us. I left the dining room before dessert was served. I didn't want to watch my brother enjoy the fruits of his labor.

I retreated to my room with a book from the library. Halfway through chapter two my brother appeared in my bedroom doorway and held up a small plate.

I scrunched my nose and stared at the dish. "What is that?"

"The other half of the mousse. It looks messy because I had to hurry before anybody saw me."

I crossed my arms and turned my head away, not wanting to be tempted. "Take it away. I only want it if I've earned it."

"We worked hard," he countered. "We both earned it."

"I didn't work hard enough or I would've won."

"I saw you. I know you could've beaten me."

"Nonsense." I refused to look at him. Nathaniel knew me better than anyone. He'd see the truth written on my face. "And if I had won, I certainly wouldn't be sneaking in your room to offer you any of my victory. That's a weakness, little brother. You should work on that."

"I don't like competing with you. I wish they would stop forcing us."

"They're only trying to make us better."

"Better for what? Aren't we good enough as we are? Why not just let us *be*?"

Why did my brother have to be so contrary? We were the children. It was our job to learn from our parents and be obedient. It didn't matter how we felt about it. Our feelings had no place in training. It was all about power and control. I deserved to lose today when I failed to exercise both.

"Get out of my room, Nathaniel. If I have to say it again, I'll turn you into a worm." I imbued my glare with extra venom. "And you know I'll do it."

"It doesn't have to be like this, Hyacinth," he said in a quiet voice.

I turned my attention back to the book and heard the sound of soft footsteps as he retreated. Only when the sound dissipated did I curl into a ball on the bed and let myself cry. It was my fault I lost. I was too soft and I'd paid the price. I'd lost the chocolate mousse as well as my parents' approval.

I dried my tears and folded my hands under my cheek.

There was always tomorrow.

1

I awoke to something damp and wet on my cheek. Until I touched it, I assumed it was a leaf that had somehow blown through the window. Leaves, however, were not furry.

I bolted upright to see an aging Yorkshire terrier on my bed. "PP3, why are your paws wet?" Prescott Peabody III was getting up there in dog years and I had a sickly moment where I worried that incontinence had gotten the better of him.

"Sorry, Mom." My daughter Marley poked her head into the bedroom. "He was whining to go out so I took him while you were sleeping. I guess it rained during the night because the grass is wet."

Either that or Aunt Hyacinth did a spell to turn the cottage grounds into a swamp. I wouldn't put it past her.

"I guess it has to rain on occasion or the grass wouldn't be so green," I said. The town of Starry Hollow was contained within a magical weather bubble which meant the weather was almost always perfect.

PP3 licked my cheek and panted. Basic physical activity was an exertion for the little dog these days.

I looked at Marley. "What time is it? Shouldn't you be leaving for school?"

"I'm leaving a little later today because I'm getting a ride from Jinx."

I sat up and wiped the sleep from my eyes. "Who's Jinx? Sounds like a cat."

"Fern Green-Wart. She's two years ahead of me at school."

"That's an unfortunate name."

"Duh. Which is why she goes by Jinx."

I stretched my arms over my head. "She's old enough to drive?"

"Not yet. She's picking me up on her broomstick, not in a car."

I cast a quick glance at her. Marley had a fear of heights and didn't like to fly. "And you're okay with that?"

"I want to be."

I wasn't about to argue. I would love for Marley to overcome her fear and embrace flying. "Since when do you get rides to school from upperclass students?"

"Since Jinx offered and I didn't want to say no. She's extremely good at math *and* mixology."

"A rare breed." I swung my legs over the side of the bed and stifled a yawn. "What time do you leave then?"

"Twenty past seven." Marley checked the clock on her phone. "Which is in two minutes."

My eyes popped. "Wait, what? It's almost seven-thirty?"

"Yes, why?"

I sprang to my feet and bolted for the bathroom. "I have a board meeting in ten minutes."

"Who schedules a meeting for seven-thirty in the morning?"

"The sadistic matriarch of our family, that's who," I called over my shoulder.

Marley followed me to the bathroom door. "Does she know you're coming?" 'She' was Aunt Hyacinth, family matriarch and bane of my existence. Or maybe I was the bane of hers. It was hard to tell the difference.

I stuck a toothbrush in my mouth. "Do I look insane to you?"

"Look in the mirror and ask that question again."

I glanced in the mirror at my unruly dark hair, oily T-zone, and a toothbrush protruding from my mouth. "Point taken." I brushed and spit. "I'm going to ambush her. Ask forgiveness, not permission."

Marley studied me. "Are you sure you're not just pushing her buttons by showing up?"

I poured mouthwash into a small cup and dumped it in my mouth.

"Absolutely not," I said, although it sounded more like 'abooltleenut' because my mouth was full of minty goodness. I spit and rinsed. "I'm a Rose and I have a place on the board of the Rose Foundation the same as everybody else in the family."

"And when I'm eighteen, I'll have one, too?"

"If you want it, yes."

"Wear your battle armor," she warned. "Aunt Hyacinth won't be pleased to see you."

"The feeling is mutual."

Ever since Aunt Hyacinth ordered Alec Hale, my boss and boyfriend, to fire me from the weekly paper she owned, tensions had been high between us. I ended my relationship with Alec and started a new business venture with my familiar Raoul, an agency called R&R Investigations. Business was slow but that was to be expected at this stage.

A horn honked outside.

"She has a horn on her broomstick?"

Marley smiled. "Pretty cool, right?"

"You and I have different definitions of cool."

Marley blew me a kiss. "Good luck!"

"Same to you. I want to talk about this Jinx character when you get home."

"She's not a character. She's my friend."

"You know what I mean. This is the first I'm hearing about her and she's giving you rides to school." I didn't know why I bothered finishing the sentence. Marley was already gone.

Still on the bed, PP3 wagged his tail and settled on my pillow.

"Great. Now there will be a wet butt mark where my head goes."

I ran a brush through my hair and dressed. A shower would have to wait.

Thankfully, the meeting was held in the massive family home known as Thornhold, which meant I only had to dash across the grounds to get there. I would've flown but I didn't want my hair to get tangled. It would only give my aunt more ammunition to use against me.

Simon greeted me at the door with a bemused expression.

"What? I'm here for the meeting." I brushed past him.

The butler made a noise at the back of his throat. "I'm sure my lady will be pleased to see you've retained an interest in the family's philanthropic endeavors."

"Oh, stuff it, Simon. You know she'll be peeved. Better fetch the smelling salts now and get ahead of the situation."

He bowed slightly. "I might also mix a vodka tonic in case she requests her morning medicine."

"I'll save you time. You go play bartender and I'll show myself to the boardroom."

"As you wish."

I hurried to the wing of the house where the meeting was currently in progress. Everyone was in attendance this morning, even Wyatt Nash, the werewolf formerly married to my cousin Linnea. In a way I was glad he'd graced us with his presence. It would be challenging for Aunt Hyacinth to be laser-focused in her anger at me when Wyatt was there to draw her ire. Divide and conquer. If only Napoleon had been blessed with aggravating family members that refused to bow to his demands, he might never have risen to power.

I slipped into the empty seat behind Wyatt as my aunt raised her gaze from the table. Our eyes locked. I knew things were bad when the look I got was one wrinkle worse than the look Wyatt usually received upon entry. The werewolf wasn't even wearing shoes today. He'd removed his boots and placed his stocking feet on the table, showing off the hole through which his big left toe now protruded. A class act, as always.

"Ember," my aunt said in a voice cold enough to freeze the pitcher of water on the table. "We weren't expecting you today."

I noticed she wore one of my favorite kaftans—the emerald green fabric was covered in white cats modeled after her familiar, Precious.

"I'm not sure why not. I'm a Rose, same as the rest of you." I glanced at Wyatt. "Well, most of you."

Wyatt whistled. "Never thought I'd see the day when the golden girl was knocked down a peg under me."

"I was never the golden girl," I hissed. More like the goose who laid the golden Marley.

"I don't recall including you on the email for this meeting." My aunt's gaze searched the room in an effort to root out the guilty party.

I maintained a casual air. "I receive all the emails. Regardless of your personal feelings, I am still a member of the board."

"She's not wrong," Florian interjected. "She has as much right to be here as any of us."

Aunt Hyacinth sniffed. "I think that might be an overstatement."

Simon bustled in with a cocktail glass and set it in front of Aunt Hyacinth, as well a second glass filled with juice. Ah, the old orange juice chaser.

Simon bowed. "Your morning medicine, my lady."

Wyatt snickered. "I'm feeling a little unwell. Maybe I could get one of those, too."

Aunt Hyacinth ignored him. "Thank you, Simon. That will be all."

"I have a question." My cousin Aster tied her signature white-blond hair back in a sleek ponytail as she spoke. "Why did you schedule this meeting at the same time the twins need to be taken to preschool? You know our daily routine."

My aunt looked affronted. "Because everyone gets busy during the day. I assumed an early morning start would be best for all of us."

"Couldn't you get Sterling to drive the boys?" Linnea asked.

I was interested in Aster's response. Her husband Sterling was meant to be making an effort to be more accessible to the family and that included chauffeur duty for their twin sons, Ackley and Aspen.

"He did drive them, but it made our morning unnecessarily hectic because I had to get ready to come here, which meant I couldn't help with the twins."

Aunt Hyacinth forced a smile. "The sooner we all stop complaining, the sooner we can finish this meeting."

Florian raised his pen in the air. "I didn't complain. Can I start with something important?"

"What's that?" Wyatt asked. "The payments on your yacht are behind and you want to know who Mommy can call on your behalf?"

Florian glared at his former brother-in-law before shifting his focus to Aunt Hyacinth. "I want to remind everyone that Natural Selection begins filming this week. It may not be a big deal to you personally, but it's a big deal for Starry Hollow and I need things to run smoothly."

"*We* need things to run smoothly," Aster added.

Both Florian and Aster were members of the tourism board and took their roles seriously.

Aunt Hyacinth folded her hands and regarded him. "And how can we assist you with that? Tie Ember to a flag pole until the production has finished?"

Wyatt leaned back to look at me and chuckled. "You're really deep in it. I've been the one tied to that flag pole. I don't envy you."

"This isn't directed at anyone in particular," Florian said. "It's just a general statement."

"Where will filming take place?" Linnea asked.

"All around town for the dates. I'm trying to get them to showcase as much of the town's charms as possible so that viewers will want to come here."

"How disappointing I'll be away and miss all the fun," Aunt Hyacinth murmured into her cocktail.

I perked up. "You're going out of town?" That was unusual.

"Yes. Simon is taking his annual leave and I've decided to take advantage of his absence. Precious will be joining me."

I snorted. My aunt was so accustomed to being waited on that she'd decided to go elsewhere to be pampered during her butler's vacation.

She leveled her son with a look. "Need I remind you, Florian Rose-Muldoon, no parties."

The wizard held up a hand as though swearing an oath. "I wouldn't dream of it."

"Where's everyone staying during filming?" Linnea asked. "I don't have anyone booked from the show that I'm aware of."

Florian tapped the end of his pen on the table. "Kristoff—that's the executive producer—he rented a big house for the contestants. That's how it works. They go elsewhere for dates and activities, but the main action and the selection ceremonies take place at the house and there's a camera crew there."

"What's a selection ceremony?" Wyatt asked.

"It's where the male chooses his potential mates," Florian replied. "Each episode, one woman gets a special date and one gets eliminated until there are only two left to choose between in the final ceremony."

Wyatt's ears twitched. "And then they fight to the death?"

Florian reeled back, appalled. "No."

Wyatt folded his arms and smirked. "What's the problem? That would get more ratings than whatever you're about to say. Maybe I'll start a werewolf version. I'll call it Be My Alpha."

I resisted the urge to roll my eyes, unlike the rest of the family whose eyeballs were working overtime this morning.

"Do they at least have a threesome?" Wyatt pressed.

Florian wore a lopsided grin. "I wouldn't be opposed to suggesting it."

Aster smacked the back of her brother's head.

Aunt Hyacinth's lips formed a straight, thin line. "Basically you've invited pornography to Starry Hollow."

Linnea slid the cocktail glass closer to her mother. "How do you know which women get chosen? Does he just read a list? Because that sounds dreadfully boring."

Florian glanced at her. "It's more entertaining than that. They're given a stuffed giraffe during the selection ceremony. Maybe when they win date nights, too. I can't remember the details."

Wyatt's brow furrowed. "I don't get it. What does a stuffed giraffe have to do with banging babes?"

Aster swiveled in her chair to address him. "It's the show's symbol. A giraffe represents the process of natural selection. Giraffes with longer necks better adapted to their environment. They survived and reproduced, and subsequent generations were more likely to have longer necks as well."

"If you'd paid attention in science class instead of girls, you would understand," Linnea added.

Wyatt grimaced. "So these contestants are going to have long necks? That's not sexy." He paused, nodding to himself. "Although I can think of situations where a long neck would prove useful."

Groaning, Linnea turned back toward her mother. "Does he need to be here? Can't we have our lawyer go back through the documents and find a loophole?"

Wyatt leaned forward until his lips were practically touching her neck. "Sweetheart, if I weren't here, who would make the awesome jokes?"

Linnea shuddered and rolled her chair a few inches forward.

Wyatt tipped his head back and laughed.

"If there was such a loophole, believe me, I would've used it long ago," Aunt Hyacinth said. She shot me a look. "More than once, in fact."

Marley was right about my motives, at least partially. I felt a mild thrill that my presence had unsettled the ice queen. She'd made my life miserable and I wasn't above returning the favor. Petty, table for two.

"Why is a television show so important?" my aunt grumbled. "I didn't realize anyone watched television anymore."

"Natural Selection is hugely popular," Aster interjected. "We may not like the premise, but getting them to film here is a boon for Starry Hollow. National exposure every week and all we need to do is open our doors."

Wyatt laughed. "National exposure sounds dirty."

"But will it attract the right sort of tourists? Perhaps we don't want the sort of riff-raff that find Natural Selection riveting to watch."

To the surprise of no one, Hyacinth Rose-Muldoon was even particular about the type of tourists the town attracted.

"You can't control every aspect of the town," Florian admonished her.

She squared her shoulders. "And why not? What's the point of being the unofficial leader of Starry Hollow if I can't exert my influence?"

"More tourists mean more money for small business owners like me," Linnea pointed out. "Palmetto Inn could do with more guests. Our numbers have been low lately."

"And why is that?" Aunt Hyacinth asked. "What have you done wrong?"

Linnea pressed her lips together and I could tell she was

refraining from making a comment she'd regret. I'd worn that expression more times than I cared to count.

"Business is seasonal in a seaside town like ours," Aster chimed in. "Just because our weather is generally perfect doesn't mean the rest of the world is free to come here whenever the mood strikes. They have to wait for holidays and vacation time just like Simon. Allowing the production to swarm the town now will give businesses an immediate boost, followed by another boost later once the show airs and viewers decide they'd like to see the town in person. The more locations they use to film, the better for everybody."

"I pity the house they've rented to film this monstrosity," my aunt muttered. "It will end up on every visitor's map." She shuddered and downed the remainder of her cocktail, followed quickly by the orange juice.

We continued through the agenda and I was relieved my aunt didn't direct any questions to me. I was certain she'd quiz me on my current financial situation and then gloat at my lackluster response.

Instead, she simply adjourned the meeting.

"Have a good trip," I said, rising to my feet. "Hope you get what you want out of it." Like she could ever relax. My aunt would find a way to work herself into a disapproving frenzy wherever she went.

She looked at me, unsmiling. "I fully intend to."

2

There's a problem with the trash.

I turned away from the island to regard Raoul as he climbed through the kitchen window above the sink. "What kind of problem? It stinks to high heaven? Because I've got news for you, buddy, trash doesn't smell like the bouquet of flowers you think it does."

The raccoon dropped from the counter to the floor with the elegance of a panther. No small feat with a stomach that suggested a deep love of carbs. *I think we have an uninvited guest.*

I raised my eyebrows. "Someone has the nerve to horn in on your turf? Who would be that foolish?"

He splayed his paws. *No clue, but they must be new in town. I'll have to send a message.*

"I don't think a unicorn head on the overturned lid of a garbage can is the way to go on this one."

The raccoon gaped at me. *What kind of sick mind conjures up an image like that? Sheesh.*

"It's from a movie, but I put my own spin on it. Never mind." I heaved a sigh and went back to making breakfast.

Raoul sniffed the air. *What's cooking?*

"I soaked oats overnight."

He cringed. *Why on earth would you do a thing like that? Who wants to eat mush that looks like someone regurgitated it first?*

I aimed a wooden spoon at him. "First, I'm trying to eat better and breakfast is a good starting point. Second, that's disgusting and now that you've put the idea in my head, I don't want to eat it." I stared at the rolled oats with a mixture of disappointment and disgust.

He dusted off his paws. *My work here is done. Now how about rustling up some bacon like the gods intended?*

A dog bark pierced the air and PP3 came tearing into the kitchen like someone had set his tail on fire.

"I haven't seen you move that fast since Marley dropped a piece of cheese on the floor."

The doorbell rang and I frowned at Raoul. "Did you invite someone?"

The raccoon exuded innocence. *Not me.*

I wiped my hands on my jeans and walked to the front door to open it. An elderly woman stood on the doorstep leaning on a cane carved from rosewood. Her white hair was worn in a tight bun and her floral dress skimmed her ankles. Her buckled shoes with chunky heels reminded me of the shoes I used to draw on Pilgrims in elementary school. No idea if my representation was accurate but it amused me to see the style on a living, breathing woman.

"I beg your pardon. Are you one of the 'R's in R&R Investigations?"

"That's right. I'm Ember Rose."

"Oh, good. I thought I might have the wrong address."

"This is my private home. If you'd like to make an appointment, I have an office…"

She grimaced. "That shed next to the Sheriff's Office? I don't think so." She waved airily. "This will do. It's small, but at least it wasn't designed for gardening tools."

Raoul and I exchanged glances.

"How can we help you, Ms...?"

"My name is Mrs. Evelyn Sinclair." The nymph paused for effect and I got the distinct impression she expected us to genuflect, or at least recognize the name.

I remained upright. "Nice to meet you, Mrs. Sinclair. How can we help you?"

Her brow furrowed. "We?"

I inclined my head toward the raccoon. "This is my partner, Raoul. The other 'R.'"

She seemed momentarily taken aback. "I see."

"Is that a problem?" I asked. I didn't have space for another wealthy, condescending woman in my life. I was fully stocked at the moment.

She contemplated Raoul for a brief moment. "I don't see why."

I widened the gap in the doorway. "In that case, why don't you come in?"

She crossed the threshold, using her cane for leverage.

"Would you like a drink or a bite to eat?" I offered. "I have water, coffee, or tea."

"Nothing for me, thank you."

"Why don't you tell us the reason for your visit?"

"You may have heard there's to be a television show filming in town."

"Natural Selection?"

Mrs. Sinclair nodded crisply. "Good. You know it. That saves me time on the background information." She made a sweeping gesture. "Aren't you going to invite an old woman to sit down? This cane isn't just for show." She shook her head in dismay. "What's happened to hospitality in this world? I worry for future generations."

Raoul fluffed a pillow on the sofa and gestured to the cushion.

"Hmm," Evelyn said. "I'm unaccustomed to being seated by vermin."

"Raoul isn't vermin, Mrs. Sinclair. He's my familiar."

She regarded the raccoon with renewed interest. "Is that so? Well, I don't know what that says about you, my dear." She lowered herself to the cushion, but her back remained ramrod straight. "I'm here because my grandson is the star of the show."

"Congratulations?" I wasn't sure what she expected me to say.

"Thank you. It was inevitable that they'd cast him. He's like a young Charlton Heston, with the added benefit of being a Sinclair." She cast me a sidelong glance. "Surely you've heard of us?"

For a brief moment, it was like staring at Aunt Hyacinth sans the kaftan. "Um, I'll be honest. I don't follow...bloodlines because I don't...care?"

Evelyn ignored my response. "Sheridan Sinclair is not going to marry some gold-digging floozy on my watch."

"No, it'll be on the watch of three million viewers, if the numbers are to be believed."

Raoul stifled a laugh. *Good one.*

"If you don't want him to marry one of the contestants, then why is he doing the show?"

She scoffed. "He signed the contract without consulting me first. I'm only his grandmother. What do I know?"

I was fluent in sarcasm, so I recognized the tone. "What is it you'd like us to do? Background checks on the frontrunners?"

She looked me up and down. "No, my dear. I'm sure they're full of skeletons. Those willing to put their lives on display are far more likely to have secrets. It's one of life's strange quirks. No. I'd like *you* to enter the competition."

I choked back laughter. "You expect me to compete in a dating competition against nubile young women and win?"

I don't think she did her research before coming here, Raoul added.

"You should know I've given birth and have the stretch marks to prove it." The marks of motherhood did not make for sexy television.

"I'm hiring you to go undercover and disrupt the competition, Ms. Rose. I don't care how you do it, but if my grandson is going to put a ring on it, I want to make sure that 'it' is you."

For a second I thought I'd misheard her. "I'm sorry. You want me to *marry* your grandson?"

She flicked a finger. "Oh, please. Absolutely not, unless it's part of the contract, in which case you'll have it annulled within days of the event. I'll be paying you a handsome fee. Handsome enough that you won't be tempted to actually stay married to him," she added pointedly.

I motioned in the general direction of Thornhold. "As you can see, I'm all set in the wealth department. I have no interest in raiding your family's piggybank." It wasn't entirely truthful, but I didn't want her to look at me as acquisitive.

"Ah, you're one of *the* Roses. I thought so because of the cottage's location and your name, of course, but it's good to be certain."

Evelyn Sinclair and Hyacinth Rose-Muldoon would either be best friends or mortal enemies.

"What if your grandson doesn't choose me? What if he actually falls in love with one of the other women?"

She snorted. "You're joking. None of these women will be worthy of him. I don't care how good they look in a swimsuit or how much they want world peace."

"I think you might be confusing the show with a beauty pageant."

"It's all the same, my dear. Women parading themselves like livestock to be milked and humped."

Raoul's eyes widened. *Milked and humped? Now that's a show I'd watch.*

"It's embarrassing," the older woman continued. "The least I can do is prevent Sheridan from making a grave mistake."

"Isn't that part of adulthood, though? Making your own mistakes and learning from them?"

She gave me a withering look that rivaled my aunt's. "We're not talking about broken hearts or dividing a music collection. Sheridan's mistake could cost him the family fortune. That will happen over my dead body."

Judging from the lines on her face, she wasn't that far off.

"I'm not sure I'm the right one for the job, Mrs. Sinclair."

"Presumably you trawled the bars for free drinks in your younger years. Channel that kind of energy."

"Actually, I was too busy being a wife and mother to bar hop."

Her eyes narrowed. "You don't have experience dating?"

"Very little. Most of my experience has been here in Starry Hollow." And I really didn't want to travel down that particular memory lane.

"I think you can manage, my dear. You seem very capable. I'm willing to do whatever it takes to keep Sheridan from making a mistake. If that means hiring you and deceiving him, then so be it."

"Aren't the contestants already chosen? What makes you think I can get in at the last minute?"

Her smile reeked of self-satisfaction. "As I understand it, you have connections with the show. I'm sure you'll figure out a way."

I take it back, Raoul said. *She has done her research.*

Mrs. Sinclair pulled a wad of bills from her purse and tossed them onto the coffee table. "Your deposit. You'll get the other half when the job's been completed."

At a glance I could see the deposit was generous. Raoul reached for the cash, but I stopped him. We didn't want to appear desperate.

I tried to recall where Florian said the production would take place but fell short. "Where do I need to go?"

She angled her head toward the door. "Thornhold. That ought to be convenient for you."

I choked on laughter. "Thornhold? I don't think so."

"According to my Sheridan, the original location fell through, but someone offered up Thornhold at the last minute."

Good grief. And I knew exactly who that someone was.

3

By the time I arrived at Thornhold, there were six cars parked along the driveway and a truck on the lawn. If they left tire marks in the grass, there would be hell to pay later.

Florian met me in the foyer. He looked surprisingly nervous for a wizard who basically had life handed to him on an enchanted silver platter.

"Thanks for getting me a spot," I said. "I promise I won't tell." I could only imagine what Aunt Hyacinth would say if she knew her pride and joy was helping me.

"You're lucky one of the women turned out to be underaged. That's the only reason there was an opening."

I noticed two men transporting a large light down the hall. "Now for the real question—how did you persuade Aunt Hyacinth to let them film here? Why on earth would she say yes?"

"To show it off to the world, I guess," Florian said.

I examined him closely. "You didn't tell her, did you?"

His face grew pale. "What makes you say that?"

I smacked his shoulder. "Because I perfected that kind of lie in high school. Are you insane? She will turn you into a slug if she finds out."

"She's away. She'll never know."

"Until she sees her house splashed all over television."

He snickered. "Do you seriously believe Mother will watch Natural Selection—or anything else? She thinks TV is for poor people and idiots."

"She said…"

"She said no parties. This isn't a party. This is a business function."

I rolled my eyes. Now I was complicit by being a part of the production. As if she needed another reason to despise me.

"What about Simon? He'll be duty-bound to tell her."

"Simon isn't here. Besides, his attachment is to the house, remember, not the owner. His duty is technically to Thornhold."

I flicked a dismissive finger. "Puh-leeze. Like that would stop him."

Florian shifted from one foot to the other. "I've hired a team of cleaners to come in once filming is over. They'll scrub away any and all traces of the guests."

I whistled. "I've got to hand it to you, cousin. You know how to cover your bases."

"That's what the ladies tell me."

I groaned. "Save that kind of nonsense for the show."

He urged me to the right. "Speaking of the show, nearly everyone's in the ballroom already. You need to get in there and stake your territory."

"My territory? I'm a tiger now?"

"You want to win, don't you?" Florian looked me up and down. "Maybe you don't. Is that what you're wearing?"

I exhaled loudly. "Thanks for the confidence boost."

"It's just that all the other women are dressed to impress and you're dressed to..." His gaze lingered on my modest shirt. "Balance their spreadsheets."

The front door opened and a man stepped into the foyer. He was about six-two with medium-brown hair, hazel eyes, and a build that suggested many hours in his home gym. His face was generically handsome. In the credits of a movie, his character would be called Handsome Man. There were no endearing flaws or interesting features. In a sea of chocolate marshmallow chunk, cookie dough, and brownie batter, he was vanilla—and not even French vanilla.

"Hello there," Vanilla Man said to us. "Am I early?"

Florian motioned for him to come forward. "Not at all. Come in. I'm Florian Rose-Muldoon. I represent the town tourism board."

"I'm Sheridan Sinclair. I'm the..." He paused. "The natural selector?"

They shook hands.

"Ember Rose," I said, shaking his hand next. "Natural selectee."

"Great to meet you, Ember." Sheridan took in the impressive surroundings. "Do you live here, Florian?"

"I grew up in this house, but my current home is downstairs. I have the lower floor and my mother occupies the rest of the house."

Sheridan's eyebrows crept up. "And I thought my family was wealthy."

"This house has been in our family for generations." Florian slung an arm across my shoulders and squeezed.

Sheridan's brow furrowed. "You two are related?"

"We're cousins," I said. "I don't live here, though. My place is a small cottage on the grounds."

The bachelor seemed to view me in a new light. "I didn't realize. Is that against the rules?"

"Why would it be?" I asked. "Florian isn't an official part of the production team."

Someone released a shrill whistle. "Sheridan Sinclair, are you here? We need you."

"Be right there." Sheridan cut a glance at me. "I look forward to seeing you again." He turned away and sauntered through the house.

Florian nudged me. "Did you see that? He's into you."

I laughed. "Only because he thinks I'm loaded. Guess I'd better tell him I'm out of the will."

"Don't you dare. You want to win, don't you?"

"No," I said automatically. "I mean yes. Very much. Competitive streak initiated."

He studied me. "You're not a very good actress. If you intend to win, you're going to need to improve."

"I can't help my lack of a poker face. It's from growing up in New Jersey. We don't need mouths there. Our feelings are written all over these." I circled my face with my finger.

Florian pushed my mouth wider in an attempt to form a smile. "More teeth, but not like you're constipated."

I swatted his fingers away. "I had plenty of fiber today so that's not an issue."

A couple women entered the foyer and took a few minutes to ogle the interior. Judging by their tight dresses and perfectly coiffed hair, I pegged them as competitors.

"This place is amazing," the petite blonde said. "Can you imagine living in a house like this?"

"I'd never leave," said her companion. Her light brown hair cascaded down her back and her megawatt smile was oddly energizing. It was hard not to smile back at her.

Florian cleared his throat. "As it happens, I live here."

They both turned to stare at him. Apparently they liked what they saw because two mouths curved upward in perfect synchronicity.

"Are you the guy we're competing for?" the blonde asked. She didn't seem disappointed.

"Afraid not. I'm Florian Rose-Muldoon. I work for the tourism board."

"I'm Leesa," the blonde said, "and this is Daisy. We just met this morning, but I already feel like I've known her forever."

I couldn't decide if her statement was genuine. "I'm Ember."

"I'm mesmerized," Florian added, admiring Leesa's curvaceous figure.

I coughed into my hand and said, "Honey." Honey Avens-Beech was the name of the witch with whom Florian was currently smitten and in the process of trying to win over.

Florian shot me an aggrieved look. "I think you're wanted in the ballroom, Ember."

I clasped my hands behind me. "If I am, then so are they."

"Do you two know each other?" Leesa asked.

"We're cousins," Florian said. "And not the kissing kind."

Leesa's smile widened, revealing a gap between her two front teeth. "That's a relief. It would be a shame if the hottest guy here was taken."

Daisy nudged her friend. "He just said he's not the trophy."

Leesa kept her gaze on Florian. "I don't know. He's pretty shiny."

"And I like a good polish every now and again," Florian added.

Leesa inched closer to him. "I'd be happy to rub you."

Daisy yanked her friend's arm. "Sheridan Sinclair is the trophy."

"That's his name?" Leesa asked. "Very sexy."

Daisy rolled her eyes. "Let's go before you get yourself ejected from the show. You want a giraffe, don't you?"

Leesa blew him a kiss as she was dragged away.

I shook my head at him. "And here I told Honey you might be ready to turn over a new leaf."

Florian inhaled deeply. "Old habits die hard. Besides, I can't help it if I'm catnip for women."

"Let Sheridan have the spotlight, huh? Give some other guy a chance for a change."

"You just saw Sheridan. Do you seriously think I'd be depriving him?" He urged me to the right. "Get in there before they start without you."

I hurried down the hall to the ballroom, where I encountered a familiar figure in uniform standing sentry outside the doorway.

"Good afternoon, Sheriff. This is a surprise. Are you on duty for this?"

Sheriff Granger Nash gave his shoulders a light shrug. "Somebody had to draw the short straw."

"Isn't that what deputies are for? And you've got two of them now." Recently Valentina Pitt had joined Deputy Bolan as another member of Starry Hollow law enforcement.

"I try to share the burden. Besides, this is Thornhold. Don't want anybody making off with the silver or I'll never hear the end of it from the owner."

I leaned over and whispered, "Aunt Hyacinth is away and doesn't know they're filming here."

His brown eyes widened. "That sounds like a recipe for disaster. Now I get why Florian called me." He scrutinized me. "What are you doing here, Rose? Come to watch the production in action?"

I swallowed hard. "Actually, I'm here as a contestant."

He started to cough, which quickly morphed into a choking sound. I whacked him hard between the shoulder blades.

He quickly recovered. "Why on earth would you want to do a thing like that?" He flicked a glance over his shoulder at the assembled contestants in their micro dresses and spiked heels.

"I can't tell you."

He peered at me. "You're not in some kind of trouble, are you?"

I gave an emphatic shake of my head. I didn't want to burden him with my financial woes. I'd been in this position before. I'd figure it out.

"You'd better get in there," he said. "Sounds like they're ready to go."

I patted his shoulder as I passed by and entered the ballroom. There were cameras, oversized lights, and wires scattered throughout the large room. A trio of burly men consulted with each other, ignoring me completely. I nearly tripped on an electrical cord as I started toward the group. An unfamiliar voice called my name.

"Here," I yelled instinctively.

The man with a clipboard pivoted to face me. "You're Ember Rose?"

"That's right."

He glanced at the sheet on his clipboard with a quizzical

expression. "It says here you're one hundred and twenty-five pounds."

"Does it?" Leave it to Florian to embellish the stats. "I ate a pizza last night. I'm a stress eater."

His gaze dropped to my stomach. "Got it." He offered his hand. "I'm Adrian Bailey. Producer."

"Nice to meet you."

He observed me from head to toe. "I think we can work with this. Offer the viewers an alternative to the usual supermodel fare." His smile slowly spread. "Yes, I can definitely see you as a contender."

"As if," a woman said.

I cut a sideways glance at her. The woman's copper-colored hair was pulled into a high ponytail and her makeup...well, I wanted to make fun of it but the truth was that it was flawless. "Sorry, what did you say?"

The woman pinned her gaze on my modest shirt. "You're no more a contender than my mom."

I smiled. "Then I guess I'm one less competitor for you to worry about. What's your name?"

"Alyx Newsome. That's A-l-y-x."

"And what do you do for work, Alyx with a 'y'?"

She inclined her head toward the camera crew. "This."

"This? Display yourself on a shiny hook in the meat market?"

"If that's what it takes to be on television."

I frowned. "So you're not here because you want to marry the guy? You just want to be famous?"

She snorted. "Duh. I'm pretty sure that's why ninety-nine percent of us are here. Isn't that right, Adrian?"

The producer shrugged. "You might be off by a percentage point."

A leprechaun strode into the room and clapped his

hands aggressively. He wore a green Kangol hat and a long-sleeved shirt in a matching shade of green that was only slightly darker than his skin. His two front teeth protruded ever so slightly. It wouldn't surprise me to learn he had a werebeaver somewhere in his ancestry.

"Welcome, everyone. I'm Kristoff Mink and I am the executive producer of Natural Selection. Every detail of this show starts and ends with me."

The contestants gathered in front of him. A few of them stood with pouty lips, chests thrust out, and hands on hips like they were having their photos taken on the red carpet. Their poses looked out of place in the stuffy, wood-paneled ballroom of Thornhold. If there were a portrait of Aunt Hyacinth on the wall, she'd be staring down at the women with disdain.

Kristoff looked sideways at Adrian. "Everybody here?"

His head bobbed emphatically. "Yes, boss. All eight. Sheridan's getting hair and makeup done in the next room."

Kristoff's gaze swept over us. "Perfect. We're going to film Sheridan's entrance in a few minutes, so let's make sure you're all camera-ready." His gaze fell on me and he snapped his fingers. "Delilah, we need a little help with this one."

A fairy fluttered into the room and immediately zeroed in on me. "I haven't seen a nose that shiny since Rudolph." She attacked my face with a brush and powder. "This will help you look less like a vampire." She turned and smiled at the woman next to me. "No offense, Bianca."

"That's okay." The woman's red lips curved into a sultry smile as she regarded me. "I'm beginning to like my chances."

I flashed a smile. "Consider me a dark horse."

Delilah clucked her tongue. "Be nice, ladies. You're all in this together."

Bianca popped a hand on her hip and raised her voice. "Listen up, ladies. For the record, I am not here to make friends. I'm here to win. That means I'm not interested in your sob story about your broken heart or your fractured family or the beloved pet who crossed the rainbow bridge after a valiant fight with skittles."

I blinked. "Skittles?"

Bianca waved a hand airily. "Whatever disease. Who cares?"

"Skittles is a type of candy, not a fatal disease."

Bianca gave me with a withering look. "I guess you're meant to be the smart one. Figures."

"Smart mouth, maybe. Not so sure about the rest of me."

Alyx raised her eyebrows. "Did you just manage to insult yourself *and* compliment yourself at the same time? Impressive."

Kristoff snapped his fingers over his head. "One, two, three. All eyes on me, darlings." He motioned for Delilah to take flight and she vacated the room. "Cameras are about to roll. I'm going to introduce Sheridan and then he'll ask each of you a couple questions. Depending on your answers, he'll decide which one of you he'd like to spend extra time with first. You'll have to earn it. Your opportunity to get to know him won't be handed to you."

I raised my hand. "Do we get to ask him questions, too?"

Kristoff appeared taken aback. "Why would you do that?"

I glanced at the curious faces surrounding me. "To get to know him," I said slowly.

Bianca glared at me. "Have you never watched this show before?"

"Afraid not."

Disregarding my question, Kristoff adjusted his hat. "How about it, ladies? Are you ready to meet your future husband?"

The lights brightened and it took a minute for my eyes to adjust. The camera focused on Kristoff as he gave his opening spiel about the rules of Natural Selection. I spent most of the time checking out the competition, or the so-called floozies that my client was so worried about. To be fair, they weren't dressed like scientists and professors, but I wasn't willing to judge them based on their appearance for a television show. They were here to marry the guy, not perform brain surgery on him.

"And here's this season's apex predator you all want to mate with—meet Sheridan Sinclair." Kristoff gestured to the ballroom doorway.

Apex predator seemed like the wrong analogy but it didn't seem wise to correct the executive producer in the middle of filming.

Sheridan Sinclair strutted into the room like a peacock with one-of-a-kind feathers. "It's so great to meet you all." His eyes darted left to right. He seemed uncertain where to look first until his gaze landed on Daisy. Like me, he immediately got caught in the magnetic glare of her smile.

The women called out flirtatious responses. I stayed silent, waiting to see how the game was played before I waded in.

"Sheridan is going to ask questions and you'll each get a chance to respond," Kristoff explained. "But you'll only get thirty seconds so choose your words wisely."

That might be a tough ask for some of these women.

Sheridan positioned himself in the center of the room and we fanned out around him. "It's important to be resilient in this world. That's how we endure as a species and help the next generation to thrive. To that end, I'm looking for a mate with impressive survival skills." He slotted his fingers together. "Hit me with an example of how you've overcome adversity in your life."

I didn't expect questions with any depth and instantly regretted my lack of preparation.

A brunette in a tight yellow dress was the first to step forward. "Hi, Sheridan. I'm Jackie. It's so amazing to meet you. You're very hot." She had the kind of wild eyes that plagued Claire Danes aka Carrie Mathison on the TV show *Homeland*.

"Thank you, Jackie. You're not so bad yourself. What's the adversity you've had to overcome?"

"I constantly have to overcome the fact that people think I'm crazy," Jackie said.

Sheridan wore a bemused expression. "And why does everybody think that?"

"Probably because I act crazy." She held out her hands in a placating manner. "But I'm not, I swear. I don't want you to think I am."

"If you have to insist you're not crazy on the regular," Bianca whispered, "it suggests otherwise."

I didn't disagree.

"I guess that's an example of overcoming adversity," Sheridan said, although he didn't sound convinced.

The petite blonde I'd met in the foyer stepped forward next. "I'm Leesa. It's so nice to meet you. I love your teeth. They're so perfect. I'd love to see how easily they take off my bra."

His brow lifted. "Well, that's...Yeah, me too."

The other women shot daggers at Leesa's back.

"I totally understand adversity, Sheridan. My sorority

had three brunettes." Leesa held up three fingers. "We had to work so hard to convince the fraternities that we were still the best one to mix with. It was hard, let me tell you, especially when you're the social chair."

He stared at her blankly for a moment before recovering. "That's..."

"Idiotic?" I offered under my breath.

Bianca moved in front of Leesa and fluttered her eyelashes at Sheridan. "I'm Bianca and you are more attractive than I dared to imagine."

Sweet baby Bianca. Where did that infantile voice come from? When Bianca spoke to us earlier, she sounded like the femme fatale in a film noir who was puffing on her fifth cigarette in an hour. Now she sounded like she'd sucked all the helium out of a balloon.

Sheridan seemed to like what he saw because his smile broadened. "Why don't you tell me about your struggle with adversity, Bianca?"

"I had to attend my safety school. It was tragic, but I still managed to graduate with honors and field multiple job offers during a weak economy."

"And which school was that?"

"Tulane."

Sheridan brightened. "Oh, wow. That's a great school, and I love New Orleans. One of my favorite places to party."

"I'd be more than happy to show you around, but I doubt we'd manage to leave the hotel room." She gave him a seductive wink before turning to the group with a triumphant smile.

A statuesque woman took the opportunity to respond next. "I'm Ashley and I'm a yoga instructor who loves monarch butterflies and meditation. I'd love to share with you a moment of adversity I faced on my journey toward self-actualization."

Only monarch? What was wrong with other types of butterflies?

His brow creased as he seemed to absorb her words. "And I'd love to hear about it, Ashley." Although his response seemed patient and polite, it still felt forced. My gut told me that Sheridan would like nothing more than to roll his eyes and tell her to nama-don't-ste.

Alyx was next, followed by Daisy. Alyx talked about her experience as a mixed species, which made me like her more than I did initially. Daisy told a story about overcoming challenges during preparation for a skating competition where she won the gold medal despite competing with a broken foot.

Then it was my turn.

"I'm Ember Rose from New Jersey," I began.

Sheridan wore a sympathetic expression. "Oh, wow. That must've been awful for you."

I blanched. "That's not my adversity story. I was only giving you the background."

He grew flustered. "Oh. Please, continue."

I told my story about Jimmy the Lighter, the mobster who tried to kill me, and the whirlwind trip to Starry Hollow courtesy of my cousins.

Everyone gaped at me.

"That must've been intense," Sheridan said. He was gazing at me with a mixture of curiosity and interest. Take that, Charles Darwin.

"Oh, it was." I recognized the opportunity for a double entendre, but I couldn't bring myself to do it. I wasn't interested in Mr. Vanilla. Then I remembered I was being paid to capture his interest. Before I could remedy my lack of a saucy answer, the final woman crossed the room until she was mere inches away from him.

"I'm Tish and, if you don't mind being alone with me in a dark room, I'll tell you my story in private." Tish linked arms with Sheridan and guided him out of the ballroom.

The rest of us stared at each other in confusion as one of the cameramen followed them.

"What just happened?" Daisy asked.

"Tish is playing hardball," Leesa said. "That's what happened."

A frown marred Daisy's pretty features. "Who does that?"

"Someone who wants to win at any price," I said.

Bianca pivoted to Kristoff. "Are you going to let that happen?"

"I think *you* let that happen," he shot back. "This is Natural Selection, Bianca. You need to do a better job of guarding your territory."

"Like what? Pee around the perimeter of the room?" Leesa asked.

My eyes widened. I could only imagine Aunt Hyacinth's horror at the stench of urine emanating from her ballroom.

"We're still rolling in here," Aidan said from the shadows.

Kristoff reclaimed our attention from the center of the room. "There are categories we'll explore during the course of the show. Reproduction. Heredity. Variation in fitness or organisms."

Leesa raised her hand. "Variation? Is that like whether you have multiple or how long it takes you?"

It took me a minute to understand the confusion. "Organisms," I emphasized.

She smacked her cheek. "Oh! Forget it."

"Variation in characteristics," Kristoff continued without missing a beat. I had a feeling he was accustomed to inane questions.

Tish and Sheridan returned to the ballroom with the cameraman trailing behind them. I noticed pink lipstick smeared on his cheek. It seemed that Tish managed to sneak in the first kiss. The other women were none too pleased.

"That's not fair," Daisy complained.

Kristoff shrugged. "Nothing's fair about Natural Selection. That's the nature of the beast."

"Survival of the fittest," Tish said with a Cheshire cat smile.

"More like survival of the flirtiest," Leesa fumed.

Sheridan rubbed his hands together. "This first meeting has been awesome. Kristoff, I am more than ready to meet my future wife."

Kristoff beamed at us. "That's great news, Sheridan. Now, which potential mate would you like to choose for extra quality time?"

"You mean a date?" Jackie asked.

"No, that's next time," Kristoff explained. "This is simply an extra twenty minutes of getting to know each other."

Sheridan's eyes skimmed over us. "Tish."

Tish blew him a kiss. "Looking forward to it, babe."

The other women struggled to contain their disappointment. Daisy looked like she was on the verge of tears. I got the sense most of these women were accustomed to getting their way, which explained their failure to drum up decent adversity stories.

Kristoff's hand sliced across his neck and the lights cut. "Let's get set up in the living room for the quality time segment. Delilah, touch up Tish and Sheridan's hair and makeup."

Sheridan wiped his brow. "How was it? Did I look good? I mean, I felt good, but it's hard to tell."

Tish fluttered her eyelashes. "You look more than good. Taste good, too." She ran her tongue over her top lip in a seductive fashion.

"Who else hates her already?" Daisy whispered.

The rest of the women held up their hands. Let the games begin.

4

I was relieved Kristoff agreed to let me sleep in my own home during production because of Marley and PP3. It helped that Rose Cottage was nestled in the bosom of Thornhold and I could easily travel back and forth for filming. I had to admit, though, the thought of sleeping in Aunt Hyacinth's house without her knowledge was somewhat enticing. She would plotz if she knew how many strangers were milling around her mansion right now. Not only strangers, but strangers she'd wholeheartedly disapprove of. Not a legacy in sight, except Sheridan.

Marley popped her head into my bedroom, where I was currently changing into pajamas. "How was it?"

"As weird as you'd expect."

She sat on the edge of my bed and bounced. "Any other witches?"

"No, why?"

She shrugged. "Just curious."

I eyed her curiously. "No, you're not. You know something."

Marley fell back on the bed and splayed her arms like she was making a snow angel. "Okay, I know something."

I adjusted the elastic waistband of my pajama bottoms. "Spill it."

"I researched previous shows and, statistically, a witch has the best chance of winning."

I sat beside her on the bed. "Is that so?"

"Out of twenty shows, a witch was selected as the final recipient of Darwin eleven times."

"Who's Darwin?"

"The stuffed giraffe. That's his name."

"I didn't realize he had a name."

Marley rolled to face me. "If you intend to win, you really need to up your game. That means research."

"The other women can't control their species, though, can they? Give me data I can use."

"Good point." She drew herself back to a seated position. "Sheridan Sinclair is a nymph. He's likely to respond positively to woodland smells. Wear lotion with scents like patchouli and cinnamon."

"What about the smell of seafood?"

"He's not a water nymph."

"How many of the bachelors have been nymphs before him?" Maybe nymphs tended to choose vampires or other species over witches.

"Four. They're not a popular species for television."

"Let me guess, most bachelors have been vampires."

She nodded. "Followed quickly by werewolves."

I grunted. "Sounds about right."

PP3 trotted into the room. I scooped the aging dog off the floor and set him on the bed. He immediately marched over and rubbed his butt on my pillow before curling into a ball.

"Now that's what I call gratitude." I'd have to flip over the pillow before I put my head on it later.

"I told Jinx you were competing in the show."

I smiled. "And now I'm the coolest mom ever?"

"No, she asked whether you suffered from low self-esteem or unresolved childhood trauma."

"What did you tell her?"

"I couldn't tell her the real reason you agreed to do the show, but she isn't wrong about the childhood trauma part." She flipped a long strand of hair off her face. "Do you think I'm destined for self-esteem issues because of my unresolved childhood trauma?"

I joined her on the bed so we were nose-to-nose. "I feel like we communicate about our feelings in a healthy way. Do you think it's unresolved?"

She shrugged. "I guess. We don't talk much about Dad, though."

"I suppose that's true, but it's not because I'm deliberately avoiding the topic." My life with Karl just seemed very far away. Sometimes it was as though that history belonged to someone else and I merely had access to the files.

"I know, but it would be nice to hear more stories, when you think of them. No rush."

"I will make an effort. I promise." I booped her nose.

"Alec's coming to school this week."

My heart stuttered. "Alec Hale?"

"No, Alec Baldwin." She rolled her eyes. "Yes, Alec Hale."

I propped my head up in my hand and leaned on my elbow. "That was quite the abrupt change in topic."

"Not really. We were talking about trauma."

I glowered at her. "My issues with Alec are resolved and

you know it. Is he speaking about his books or the newspaper?"

"His books. The school librarian organized it. She's a big fan, too."

"Are you nervous about seeing him?" Marley and Alec adored each other, which was one of the hardest things about our breakup.

"No. I can hide in the crowd if I really want to. I already know which tall kid I can sit behind if necessary."

I smiled. "Such a strategic thinker."

"Failing to plan is planning to fail."

My head swiveled left to right. "Did I inadvertently wander into a TED Talk?"

Marley didn't crack a smile. "I do miss him, though."

"Of course you do. It's only natural." I planted a kiss on her forehead. I missed him, too, but not because I wanted him back. It was more that I missed the relationship that could've been. The one I'd truly believed we were capable of. I'd made peace with the fact that it wasn't meant to be. To paraphrase a cute sign I saw on Etsy, the past is where I learned the lesson; the future is where I apply it.

Or the present.

"Jinx wants his autograph, though, so I may have to help her out."

"If he's showing up at school, I think he'll be amenable to signing books without your intervention."

"Do you want me to pass along a message?"

I pressed my lips together. "No message, but I appreciate the thought."

My phone vibrated on the bedside table and Florian's name appeared on the screen.

"Are the ladies too noisy for you, you poor thing?" I asked. "That's what you get for inviting more than a dozen strangers to live above your man cave. Some of the crew members have hooves, you know."

Florian didn't laugh. "Could you come over?"

"Now? I just got in my pj's. Kristoff said I could sleep at home."

"It isn't that...We have a situation."

My stomach plummeted. "Let me guess. Your mom came home early and she's going full Carrie at the prom." The thought of Aunt Hyacinth melting down was both terrifying and intriguing. There was a reason the witch was at the top of the food chain in a town filled with powerful paranormals.

"Not exactly."

I sighed into the phone. "I'll be there in five minutes."

"Problem?" Marley asked as I put down the phone.

"Naturally." I debated whether to change. In the end, I decided to throw on a pair of slippers. That way I could slide straight into bed when I returned. "It's a school night. Please go to bed on time if I'm not back for some reason."

Marley cast a wary glance at me. "You're only going to Thornhold, right?"

I recognized the flare of anxiety in her blue eyes. Although she'd gotten better with age and the inheritance of magical powers, Marley still battled certain demons on occasion, including those that involved the dark and being alone. She wouldn't be watching horror movies anytime soon.

I patted her arm. "I'll be a stone's throw away. Besides, I'm going in my pajamas. It's not like I intend to hang around. Whatever Florian's emergency is, I'm sure it can be handled with a quick cleaning spell." Knowing my cousin, he'd been wooing one of the contestants and spilled red wine on the carpet. "You can keep your wand under your pillow if it makes you feel better."

She brightened. "Good idea."

I gave her another kiss, this time on the cheek. "See you in a bit. I'll make sure to come in and say goodnight."

I hurried downstairs and grabbed my broom to avoid the long walk across the grounds. I could've driven, but a broomstick was fuel efficient. It also helped that I loved to fly.

The exhilaration lasted all of forty seconds because that was the time it took to fly from my driveway to Thornhold's. Still, it was an extremely pleasant forty seconds.

There were only a couple vehicles in the driveway. It seemed most of the guests decided to check out what Starry Hollow had to offer. Maybe they'd even carpooled. I briefly wondered whether I should've made an effort to bond with some of the women.

I opened the front door and shouted Florian's name. It seemed odd not to be greeted by Simon in the foyer. I hoped he was enjoying his vacation. The gods knew he deserved it.

"In here!" Florian's voice rang out.

The sound came from the kitchen. I padded through the doorway in my slippers and ground to a halt at the sight of a body on the floor. A halo of golden hair floated around her head.

"What did you do?" I whispered.

"Nothing, I swear. I came in here for a bottle opener and found her like this."

I crouched down for a better view. I instantly recognized the slightly upturned nose and the puffy lips. "It's Tish."

"One of the contestants?"

I nodded. "She's the one that snuck in the first kiss." Nobody was happy with her, except maybe Sheridan. Apparently there was an unwritten code of conduct and Tish had breached it. It was like my sophomore year when Melissa Mahone showed up at school in the same outfit as Denise Krakowski. Nobody was allowed to wear the same clothes as 'the Krak.' Her motto was 'Krak kills' for a reason. Melissa learned her lesson the hard way. She ended up in her underwear under the bleachers of the football field, along with a black eye. I knew it was true because I was the one who found her there.

Florian stared at the lifeless body. "I have no idea how long she's been here."

"We need to call the sheriff."

"Already did. He should be here any second."

I resumed an upright position. "Is anyone else here?"

He shook his head. "I don't think so."

"There are still cars outside."

"Some of them rode together. I overheard them talking about going for a late dinner and then to the clubs."

I glanced around the dimly lit kitchen. "Depending on when they left, she could've been killed while they were still here."

The kitchen wasn't exactly a hot spot for this particular crowd. I was fairly convinced a few of the women had never stepped foot inside one, not that I was one to talk. Even the microwave outsmarted me.

"Nothing seems out of place," I said.

There was nothing on the floor. The fancy kettle with the mahogany handle was on the stovetop. The white dish towels were hanging neatly over the oven handle.

"Are you sure she was killed?" Florian asked. "Maybe she tripped and fell."

"Killed?" a gruff voice interrupted.

I swiveled to the doorway where the sheriff now stood. "We seem to have a casualty of war."

The werewolf loped toward us. He had the best walk—it landed somewhere between a swagger and a meander—although now didn't seem like the appropriate time to mention it.

"Any ID?" he asked, slipping seamlessly into sheriff mode. He didn't even notice my pajamas and slippers.

"Her name is Tish. She's competing on the show," I told him.

He bent down to examine her. "Definitely dead. You found her?"

I pointed to Florian. "He found her, but he called me to come over."

Sheriff Nash peered at my cousin. "Why'd you call Ember?"

Florian shrugged. "I don't know. I see a dead body and she's an autodial. It's a natural response."

The sheriff stifled a laugh. "Have you met this woman before?"

"Not me," Florian said. "I probably saw her in the house at some point, but I didn't notice her particularly."

"Why not? She's a blonde," the sheriff said.

Now it was my turn to stifle a laugh.

"I have my eye on someone else," Florian said.

I folded my arms. "I really hope you mean Honey."

"Of course I mean Honey. All these women pale in comparison. Honey has it all—brains, beauty, pedigree. She's perfect."

The sheriff looked from Florian to me, appearing uncertain whether to take Florian's admission at face value.

"He's been trying to wear Honey down," I explained. "It's

like watching someone with a plastic spoon trying to chip away at granite."

The sheriff's mouth twitched. "I know how he feels."

"I didn't meet Tish one-on-one," I offered. "She was in the same room with me when we filmed the introduction. She upset the other women by stealing Sheridan away and nabbing the first kiss, and then quality time."

The sheriff turned his attention back to the body. "No blood. No bruises. No obvious cause of death. We'll have to seal the area and search the scene."

"I noticed you didn't say crime," Florian said, his expression hopeful.

"Only because I can't say for certain at this point, but we both know that healthy young women don't drop dead for no reason."

Florian clasped his hands in prayer form. "You won't shut down production, will you? There's a lot riding on this, not just for me but the town."

The sheriff nodded. "I hear you, Florian. I'll do my best, but if this turns out to be foul play, there's going to be an investigation in the middle of production whether you like it or not."

"What about the house?" Florian asked, and I heard the note of panic in his voice. "It was hard enough when they lost the first house. Can they still film here?"

"Not tomorrow, that's for sure."

"I understand." The wizard dragged a hand through his white-blond hair. "Please don't be foul play."

"Maybe she overdosed," I suggested.

"We'll find out soon enough," the sheriff said. "Did you see anyone else near the kitchen?"

"Not when I came in," Florian replied. "Nobody was

Magic & Marriage

around. As soon as they wrapped filming, everybody had a drink and then eventually left to go into town."

The sheriff faced me. "Is that why you weren't here either, Miss Big Red Heart Pajamas?"

It seemed he'd noticed my attire after all. "I went home to spend time with Marley and get my beauty sleep. Today was a lot of bright lights and peopling. I wanted to be fresh for tomorrow."

The sheriff contemplated the body. "This puts a whole new spin on 'til death do us part."

"And extinction," Florian added. "Maybe we're looking for a predator."

"Or a hyena," I said. "Aren't they meant to be vicious?"

"They work in packs like wolves," the sheriff interjected. He would know.

"Where did we get the term 'lone wolf' if wolves work in packs?" I mused.

"There's a lot that people get wrong about wolves," the sheriff replied. "A topic for another time." He squinted at me. "You didn't see Tish after filming then?"

"No, and if I had, I would've avoided her. She's...she was hardcore about winning. I wouldn't want to cross her path alone. She might've tried to eliminate me another way."

Florian glanced at the body and sighed. "Looks like somebody got to her first."

5

With production on hold today, I decided to head to my office. The charming building was courtesy of Aster's Sidhe Shed company and located on a vacant plot of land adjacent to the parking lot of the Sheriff's Office. I figured if I couldn't work for Evelyn Sinclair today, I might as well see if there was a minor job I could pick up.

On my way to the office, I stopped at the Caffeinated Cauldron for a caramel swirl latte with one pump of Help Me Universe. I should've opted for a dollop of You Sexy Thing but decided to save that one for the next day we filmed. As I waited in line, I spotted a familiar svelte figure ahead of me. Even from the back, she reeked of sophistication.

"Hey, Honey." I couldn't wait to text Florian and make him jealous.

Honey Avens-Beech twisted to regard me. Her dark hair was pinned back on the sides with a set of pearlescent combs and she wore a sleeveless pantsuit that accentuated her slender build and showed off her toned arms.

"Hello, Ember. Nice to see you again. How's everything?"

"I'm in desperate need of a latte at the moment." I didn't sleep well thanks to images of a lifeless Tish flashing in my mind. I even had a dream that involved Tish competing as a zombie. Sheridan didn't choose her because she smelled like rotting flesh, which seemed fair enough.

"You're more than welcome to go ahead of me. I'm not in a rush."

I waved her off. "Oh, no. I was being hyperbolic. I can wait." I tapped my foot impatiently.

Honey broke into a smile. "Please. I insist." She moved to stand behind me. "I understand you joined the cast of the dating show."

"Word gets around fast. I don't suppose it was Florian. He's been so busy with Natural Selection, he hasn't had time for gossip."

"Oh, I've heard plenty from Florian, although I do think he went overboard with the flock of bluebirds of happiness."

I laughed. "He serenaded you with birdsong, huh? I guess that's romantic."

"No, it was actual singing. The birds were spelled. They sang Adele's *Hello*."

Leave it to Florian. "How did you respond?"

A faint smile appeared. "I haven't yet, although just between us, he's wearing me down."

"A green light for stalkers everywhere."

Honey's laughter rang out. "Gods, I hate that he's charming. If he were a complete simpleton, I could give a firm no and forget the whole thing."

"He is charming. You're right about that. Years of practice wrapping his mother around his little finger."

Honey lowered her gaze. "To be perfectly frank, I worry he only wants me because I've said no."

"The thrill of the chase." I nodded. "That tracks."

She flinched. "You think that's what it is?"

"I don't mean to suggest you're not straight-up gorgeous and an absolute catch, but I can understand why your mind would veer in that direction. Florian hasn't exactly been committed to finding his ideal mate."

In the past he was all about rebelling against his mother's wishes. He'd matured somewhat in the time I knew him. Delphine Winter was his most serious relationship to date and I'd believed that one would go the distance. Seeing how happy Delphine was with Wren, though, I was glad her relationship with Florian ran its course. She and Wren were obviously better suited. There was another woman who seemed to have a casual thing going with Florian. From what I understood, she was more interested in the occasional sleepover rather than a full-blown relationship. Honey seemed like an intelligent, mature witch who saw Florian for who he was and still found him endearing. In other words, a perfect match.

We reached the counter and I ordered a specialty latte as well as a hot burstberry tea for Honey. We took our drinks to a nearby table and sat.

Honey drummed her fingers on the outside of the steaming mug. "What would you do in my shoes?"

I glanced under the table at her pair of black heels. "Fall over."

She smiled. "Like Florian and his charm, I've had years of practice walking in these."

"Must be comforting to know you always have a weapon on you."

"Yes, but if I reach down too quickly for the shoe, I risk pulling a muscle in my back so there's that."

I clutched my chest. "You're like a sister from another

mother." I leaned back against the chair. "I think you should give him a chance and I'm not saying that because we're related."

"Then why are you?"

An image of Sheriff Nash flashed in my mind. "Because we can change. Yes, Florian was a monster who called you Honey Avens-Beeched Whale, but he was also a teenaged boy at the time. We all do regrettable things in our youth."

She quirked an eyebrow. "Like get pregnant?"

"Oh, I don't regret that for a second. Marley is my greatest contribution to the world. I can't do any better than that." As far as I was concerned, I peaked early.

Her sculpted cheeks colored. "Sorry I didn't mean to suggest..."

I held up a hand. "No worries. I knew what you meant. My point is that Florian seems ready for a serious relationship and there's no harm in giving him a chance. If he's not for you, then at least you can part as friends unlike your school days." He and Delphine were on good terms despite their breakup, which suggested he'd matured in more ways than one.

Honey blew the steam off her tea and sipped. "I wouldn't say there's no harm. Heartbreak is a terrible thing."

My thoughts returned to Granger. "You got that right."

"Is that why you've decided to participate in the dating show? No risk of actual heartbreak?"

I smiled. "Something like that." I couldn't exactly broadcast my client's request or I risked exposure. The fewer paranormals that knew, the better.

"The guy isn't half bad. I saw his photo on the Starry Hollow website. Nice pecs."

"Maybe you should've joined the competition."

She groaned. "I have no interest in fighting over a man like he's a slab of meat. It's beneath us." She sucked in a breath. "Ooh, sorry, Ember. I just keep putting my foot in my mouth today, don't I?"

"No offense taken. My claws aren't out, although I can't say the same for the rest of these women."

"Speaking of claws, horrible news about the murder."

I froze. "Who said anything about a murder?"

"Castor said a body was found on the set. Is that not true?"

The gossip mill was as hard-working as ever in Starry Hollow. "It's true about the body, but that's all we know right now."

She cast a speculative glance at me. "You're close to the sheriff. Has he shared any details?"

"He didn't have to. I saw her with my own two eyes. Florian's the one who found her, you know."

Honey winced. "He did? Why didn't he tell me? Gods, how terrible for him."

"The worst part is that his mother doesn't know he agreed to let the production team film in her house while she's away. Nobody can ever tell her there was a dead woman in her kitchen. She'll hex Florian and everyone else involved. There won't be enough sage in the world to make her believe the kitchen is usable after that."

"She's such a formidable witch. To be honest, she's one of the reasons I've been reluctant to get involved with Florian."

My ears pricked. "Really? I thought Florian was the obstacle."

"Oh, he's definitely been the primary reason, but there's a lot of pressure that would come from a match with a Rose.

Magic & Marriage

I'm an Avens-Beech, but we're not quite in the same league." She wrapped her hands around the mug. "No one is."

"Are you worried about Hyacinth's reaction to you? Because I can tell you right now that's not an issue. She's been dying for Florian to date an upstanding witch from a reputable family."

Honey smirked at me. "Too bad she isn't as keen on you dating similar stock or we could be sisters-in-law."

Although her brother seemed like a nice wizard, I had no interest in Castor.

"She's keen. She just knows I don't care what she thinks."

"A rebel. I completely understand." She brought the mug to her lips. "Sometimes I wish I could've been more rebellious. I just don't have it in me."

"What would you have rebelled against?"

She took another sip of tea. "I don't know. Nothing exciting. I'd like to skip over pleasantries or forget to say please or thank you."

I gasped. "Forget your manners? But whatever would the neighbors think?"

"You haven't had that problem, I suppose. Growing up in New Jersey, you must've gotten away with all sorts of debauchery."

"I would have been much worse if I'd grown up under Aunt Hyacinth's thumb. As soon as she applies pressure, I instinctively resist. I can only imagine what that dynamic would've been like when I was a teenager."

"I suppose there must be a lot of pressure to win on the show."

"I'll have to let you know after more than one day of filming." The tension was palpable during that first day, but

I wasn't sure whether it would increase or decrease as women were eliminated, or stay at a similar level.

"What do you think about the other women? Could one of them have killed…?"

"Tish. Her name was Tish." Using a spoon, I scraped the remaining foam from the inside of the cup and ate it. "It's plausible. Those women are definitely in this to be the survival of the fittest."

"Yes, but murder? Not to mention you'd barely started filming. How could they decide so quickly that Tish was the one to beat?"

"She made herself a target." I grimaced. "Not that I'm blaming the victim. It's only that she alienated the other women through some brazen behavior."

"I hope the police don't shut down production permanently. Florian will be devastated. I know how hard he worked on encouraging them to film here."

I bit the inside of my cheek to keep from smiling. Honey sounded more smitten than she seemed to realize. I got the distinct impression it was only a matter of time before she succumbed to Florian's charms and agreed to a date. Now if only their good fortune would rub off on me.

Hours later I learned my hunch wasn't wrong.

"It's a miracle." Florian pirouetted his way into the kitchen of Rose Cottage.

I glanced up from the chopping board where I'd managed to mangle a carrot. It took real talent to screw up the chopping of a carrot.

"Did the sheriff determine it wasn't foul play?" I asked.

"No, even better. Honey has finally agreed to go out with me." Reaching into the fruit bowl on the counter, he pulled a purple grape off the stem and popped it into his mouth.

"Yes, I can see how a date with one woman is even better than identifying the murderer of another."

He seemed oblivious to my sarcasm. "Now I have to plan the perfect evening to make sure she agrees to a second date."

"Don't worry so much about perfection. Just be yourself. She wants to know the real you."

The wizard shot me a quizzical look. "Why do I get the sense you know something?"

There was no reason to deny it. "We might have had a chat at the coffee shop."

He flashed a broad smile. "You're the best, cousin."

"Listen, I didn't push her one way or the other. She made up her own mind." I pointed a finger at him. "I think it was the whole bluebird serenade."

Florian punched a fist into the palm of his hand. "I knew that would work. It was a stroke of genius." He finally noticed the carrot monstrosity. "What are you trying to do?"

I glanced at the crooked orange pieces. "What do you mean 'trying?'"

He means he can spot a culinary disaster from a mile away. Raoul padded into the kitchen from the pantry.

"How long have you been in there?" I asked.

The raccoon shrugged. *I was browsing.*

"It's not a window display. It's my food storage."

Forget magic. You should get a lesson on food storage. Maybe from squirrels. Or even a prepper.

I popped a hand on my hip. "And what's wrong with the pantry?"

You wouldn't survive a week during the apocalypse. You've got nothing except junk in there and a jar of olives.

"Black or green?"

Does it matter? They're olives. He clutched his neck and pretended to choke.

"Note to self. Olives on my next pizza and I won't have to share."

Florian drummed his fingers on the countertop. "What about Lighthouse for dinner?"

I'd love that, Raoul said. *Their dumpster always smells incredible.*

I glared at my familiar. "Nice but obvious," I told Florian. "Honey's probably been there a million times. Do something creative. Something that shows you've put in the effort."

Florian's shoulders slumped. "I have no idea how to do that."

"Learn more about her, then decide. And don't just do a meal. Add something special to it, like a sunset picnic on your boat where you've carefully selected the food."

Florian brightened. "I like that idea. Can I steal it?"

"Consider it yours."

Raoul cleared his throat.

I looked at the raccoon. "Are you choking or do you have something meaningful to contribute to the conversation?"

It so happens that I'm having a similar experience to Florian.

"You're wooing a woman you were mean to in high school?"

Okay, maybe not that similar. Her name is Fancy Nancy.

"She's high maintenance. Let that one go."

How do you know?

"It's right there in the name." I glanced at Florian. "Her name is Fancy Nancy."

Florian cringed.

She doesn't call herself that. It's what I call her. He fluttered his eyelids. *She's the most beautiful cat in the world.*

"You're smitten with a cat?"

Florian slapped the raccoon's back. "Interspecies relationships. You're taking a page out of my book."

She doesn't seem interested in me. I've tried to woo her, but it turns out she doesn't like maggots. He splayed his paws.

"Have you tried wooing her with something that appeals to her?" I inclined my head to Florian. "Kind of like the pearls of wisdom I was just sharing with this one."

I think her tastes are more refined than mine. She seems so sophisticated and worldly.

Now she really did sound like Honey.

"Why don't you flat-out ask her what she likes? The art of communication cannot be overstated."

She's not the best conversationalist. I do most of the talking. He hesitated. *Okay, I seem to do all the talking.*

I knew the type. "If she's fancy, why not try to win her over with a candlelight dinner? Rummage through the dumpsters at the best restaurants in town."

Raoul nodded. *I can work with that.*

"What kind of cat is she?"

A white Abyssinian. You've never seen a coat like hers. It looks so soft. I dream about running my paws through it.

"Where did you meet her?" Florian asked, trying to be a part of the conversation.

Raoul looked at him. *Tell him we met by the trash bins outside. The gemstones of her sparkling pink collar caught the starlight. I thought I was dreaming when I saw her.*

"Outside," I told Florian. I glanced back at Raoul. "Was she the trouble with the trash you mentioned the other day?"

She was indeed.

PP3 broke into a maddening bark and I glanced out the kitchen window to see who'd aggravated the Yorkshire terrier.

Florian joined me at the window. "Who is it? Please don't say Mother."

"Worse. Marigold."

He looked at me askance. "I don't think Marigold's worse than Mother."

"Only because you never had to endure her lessons in the lost art of out-of-body experiences. Let me tell you, it's a lost art for a reason."

I left the kitchen and opened the front door before she managed to knock.

Marigold darkened my doorstep in all her cheerleader-meets-drill-sergeant glory. The witch looked me up and down. "Look what the cat dragged in."

"Isn't that what I'm supposed to say?"

She brushed past me. "The cat must've dragged you in hours ago. The stench of fish is faint."

Closing the door, I spun around to face her. "What brings you to Rose Cottage?"

Florian leaned against the doorjamb with his arms folded. "Mother would not be happy to see you here."

Marigold grunted. "I could say the same to you, traitor. As it happens, I'm here on business."

"And Mother's out of town. How convenient."

I ignored my cousin. "What kind of business?"

"I'd like to hire you." She frowned. "You are taking new clients, right?"

"I am."

"I'll let you two talk shop." Florian tapped my shoulder. "We'll talk later."

The wizard left me alone with Marigold.

Magic & Marriage

"What's the job?" I asked, returning to the kitchen with Marigold hot on my heels.

"I need you to look into a disappearance." She grabbed a towel and fanned herself with it. "Sorry. Hot flash. They hit me out of nowhere."

I was stuck on the description of the job. "A disappearance? Don't you want to contact the sheriff?"

"With a high-profile murder investigation underway? How much traction do you think this will get?"

I groaned. "You've heard about the investigation?"

"Hazel told me this morning."

I sighed. There was no such thing as a secret in Starry Hollow. "Who disappeared?"

"My lawn elf, Harold. I have an uneasy feeling that he ended up as turtle soup in the cauldron of old Myrtle."

"Who's old Myrtle?"

She grabbed my arm. "You've not heard of Old Myrtle the Turtle Soup Lady?"

"No," I said slowly. "Can't say that I have."

"Once upon a time..."

"Seriously? We're starting this out like a bedtime story?"

Marigold shrugged. "You know how these rumors go. It's like your good friend, Artemis."

"I wouldn't start her story like that. I'd start it with 'when a servant boy meets an aristocratic girl and then dies an untimely death but hangs around for centuries afterward...'" Or something like that. "Anyway, you're a witch. If this Myrtle is a problem, why can't you handle it with a bit of magic?"

She blew a raspberry. "Come on, Ember. We can't all be descendants of the One True Witch with access to Ivy Rose's magical prowess."

True.

"Are you sure this isn't a pity job?"

Marigold drew back and regarded me. "Does that sound like the way I operate?"

No, it didn't. "Aunt Hyacinth won't like that you're funding my existence."

"She doesn't need to know, does she? In fact, I insist on it."

"This is a pretty big risk you're taking. She might be angry enough to curse you if she finds out."

"Then I guess that's a risk I'm willing to take. I never should've let her intimidate me into abandoning you. I'm sorry for that, Ember. Truly."

My heart squeezed. "It's okay, Marigold. I totally get it. I can't say I wouldn't have done the same in your comfortable shoes."

"You wouldn't have, Ember." Her voice grew quieter. "I know you wouldn't have."

I chewed on a crooked piece of carrot. "Why don't you tell me everything you know about Harold and I'll see what I can find out?"

Marigold beamed at me. "I knew you'd come through for me. How much do I owe you?"

I waved her off. "I'll forgo the deposit. I know you're good for it." It was easier to be generous with Evelyn Sinclair's deposit in the bank.

"That's very kind of you. Would you like to practice a bit of astral projection while I'm here? I imagine you've gotten a bit rusty without practice."

I swallowed the chunk of carrot. "I practice."

Marigold snorted. "Lying in bed and dreaming about sunbathing on a beach in the Caribbean isn't the same thing."

"It's almost as if you know me."

She shook her head. "I'll let you get back to torturing that carrot. We'll talk soon." She exited the kitchen with a spring in her step.

Eyeing the remainder of the carrot, I lifted the knife and concentrated on my target. I brought down the blade and chopped twice. The cut was smooth and the stick would've looked completely respectable on a serving platter at Thornhold. I smiled at the result.

Maybe practice did make perfect after all.

6

PP3 was thrilled I was home in the middle of the day and willing to walk him outside. The Yorkie could hardly contain his enthusiasm for every tree stump. Sometimes he had a rush of energy that made it hard to believe he was no longer a puppy.

The ring of my phone interrupted our peaceful outing. I maneuvered the device from my back pocket with one hand still on the leash.

"You there, Rose? All I hear is panting."

"It's the dog," I lied. Maybe I could stand to do a few laps around the yard in my downtime. "I assume this is a professional call."

PP3 didn't care that I was on the phone. The Yorkie tugged on his leash and pulled with the strength of two oxen. I nearly tripped over a rock but managed to hold on to both the leash and the phone. It took years of experience to avoid disaster.

"It is. Thought you'd want to hear the results of the autopsy."

"That was fast."

"It's a priority situation, wouldn't you say?"

I inhaled deeply. "Foul play?"

"I'm afraid so."

My stomach clenched. Poor Florian.

Poor Tish.

"What's the cause of death?" I asked.

"Poison. Strychnine. Pretty common stuff."

"That's good, right?" PP3 lunged and my arm nearly came out of its socket. I swallowed a whimper.

"Not really," the sheriff said. "Makes it harder to trace."

That made sense. "That's probably why the killer chose it."

"Which suggests it was premeditated rather than a crime of passion," he added.

It was a good albeit surprising point. Under the circumstances, I would've put my money on a crime of passion.

"Do you know how it got into her system?"

"We're not sure at this point. We combed the house and tested all the glasses and bottles we found. Didn't turn up anything."

PP3 stopped to sniff the base of a tree and gave my arm a much-needed rest.

"Does this mean you'll have to shut down production?" Florian would be devastated.

"The deputies and I talked it over and we decided it's best to keep things rolling. That way everybody stays in town and they keep busy. If the killer is among them, they might slip up sooner or later."

Or they might kill again. "Are you going to tell them about the murder? It might scare off some of the contestants if they think their life is at risk."

"What about you, Rose? Does it scare you off?"

"Of course not."

"Didn't think so."

"Does this mean they can resume filming in the house?"

"Oh, no. We've still got work to do in there. Mr. Mink will have to find an alternate venue for now."

That would make my commute a little longer, but it was nothing I couldn't handle.

"How about it then, Rose? Will you be my woman?"

My mouth turned to cotton. "Excuse me?"

"My woman on the inside. Be undercover to root out the killer. You're in the best position to dig for dirt without raising suspicions and we both know you can handle it."

Warmth rushed to my cheeks. "Yes, absolutely." I could balance my job for Evelyn Sinclair with my civic duty, right? Oh, and my new job for Marigold.

And my maternal obligations to Marley.

And...

Well, crap.

"How about talking to me about the other contestants over dinner tonight?"

I smiled at the phone. "Why? Planning to swoop in and console the losers? That sounds more like a Wyatt dating strategy."

He chuckled. "I figure it'll help me get a jump on the suspects. You've met these women. Help me figure out which ones to interview first."

"I haven't spent significant time with them. The production's only just started." My stomach churned as I contemplated my next words. "But dinner with you sounds good either way."

There. I said it.

"Now you're talking, Rose. I'll pick you up at seven."

I clucked my tongue. "Careful, Sheriff Nash. This is starting to sound more like a date."

"No, no. This is official business. I promise. If I pick you up, it'll give us more time to talk in the car."

I felt slightly disappointed. "Okay then. I'll see you at seven."

"This would be fun, if it weren't for the murder part. You know we make a great team."

We did.

"See you at seven," I said.

MARLEY CAST a speculative look in my direction. "Are you sure this isn't a date?"

"It's official business. He wants information on the other contestants and I'm in the best position to give him an unbiased view since we both know I don't give a hoot about Sheridan Sinclair."

Marley pointed to my face. "But you're wearing makeup. That lipstick even shimmers."

My fingers touched my lips. "Is it wrong that I want to look nice for dinner at a fancy restaurant?"

"If it's official business, why is he conducting it at a fancy restaurant? Why not a coffee shop or, better yet, his office?"

I crossed the room to join her on the sofa. "What's this about?"

She fidgeted on the cushion. "I just don't want anybody to get hurt."

My good mood evaporated. I wrapped an arm around her and squeezed. "Marley, it's not your job to worry about adult relationships. You focus on Marley."

"But your relationships affect me. If you and the sheriff get together and break up again..."

I exhaled. "I can't promise what the future holds."

She gave me a pointed look. "Exactly."

I kissed her forehead. "Life is messy, sweetheart. Always has been. It's part of the charm." And part of the pain, but I opted to omit that sentiment.

True to his word, the sheriff arrived at Rose Cottage promptly at seven. I moved past her to answer the door.

"Good evening, Sheriff Nash. You look…" Like a snack. I swallowed hard. "Dapper."

Dapper wasn't the right word and we both knew it. He wore a long-sleeved, collared black shirt, tight dark jeans, and black boots. He didn't look dapper. Great Mother of Abraham Lincoln. The werewolf looked *hot*.

I began to regret my decision to wear pants. A dress would've been better. "Maybe I should change."

His gaze raked over me appreciatively. "Are you kidding? Not a stitch, Rose. Not a single stitch." He offered his arm. "Shall we?"

I twisted to say goodbye to Marley. She made kissy faces, so I ignored her and continued outside.

"Are you going to call me Sheriff Nash all night?"

"That's your name and this is official business. Why wouldn't I?"

He patted my hand. "Point taken."

"Where are we headed?"

He opened the passenger door. "A new place. Haven't been there yet."

I buckled my seatbelt as he slid behind the wheel. "Who recommended it?"

"Valentina."

I stiffened. "Recommended as in asked you to accompany her?"

Magic & Marriage

He chuckled. "What are you worried about, Rose? You want to be the first to dine there with me?"

"No, of course not. It's not my business whether you eat in a fancy restaurant with her or any other beautiful young woman." I bit my tongue to keep myself from making one more stupid comment.

He started to drive, grinning from ear to ear. "This is going to be a fun night."

The new restaurant was called Shanti. The exterior included a small waterfall flowing into a koi pond that created a tranquil atmosphere.

"I almost feel guilty for coming here to talk about murder," I whispered as the hostess walked us to a table by the window that overlooked the pond.

She distributed two menus and walked away.

"Do you get to expense this?" I asked.

He glanced at me over the top of the menu. "Like for taxes?"

"Yeah."

"Don't know. Didn't give it any thought."

The server stopped at our table and gave us the spiel. Her name was Vanessa and she looked no older than eighteen. Despite her youth, she rattled off the specials like a pro and took our order. She even recommended a cocktail with tequila that sounded so good, I decided to go for it. I typically avoided tequila after a particularly unpleasant experience. It had been years since then and I realized the bad memory had faded.

"Tell me about this lone wolf issue," I said, kicking off the dinner conversation. "How do people get wolves wrong?"

"There's no lone wolf in terms of independence.

Someone too cool and aloof to be social. We're social creatures. If a wolf strikes out on his own, it's for a good reason."

"Like what? A change in scenery? Tired of the same forest?"

"Usually to find a mate."

We fell silent and stared at each other. Vanessa stopped by and set our drinks on the table.

He cleared his throat. "Thank you."

"Is that why Wyatt is alone most of the time? He's generally on the prowl for his next mate?"

He laughed. "I guess that's one way of looking at it. While we're on the subject of mates…"

"You want to know why I'm on the show."

He ducked his head. "It's none of my business, I know. Forget I asked."

"I'm not there because I want to marry Sheridan, I'll say that much."

"Didn't think so."

Vanessa delivered our drinks and slipped away. She seemed to sense we were having a sensitive conversation and gave us space—the sign of an excellent server.

"I watched a couple episodes of previous seasons…for research," he said. "Some of those women sleep with the guy during the competition."

I bit the inside of my cheek to keep from smiling. "How scandalous."

He took a long swig of ale. "I would hate to see you give a piece of yourself to yet another man who doesn't deserve you, that's all."

Ouch.

"I have no intention of doing that." I tasted the cocktail. Delicious. "Tell me how strychnine works." It seemed best to steer the conversation away from personal stuff.

"With a high dose, which this was, respiratory failure and brain death can happen anywhere from fifteen minutes to half an hour."

"Which fits with our timeline."

He nodded. "Like I told you, it's readily available so anybody could've brought it into the house and administered it without her knowledge."

"Which is why you want to discuss the women in detail." I followed another sip of the cocktail with a mouthful of water. I wanted to stay sharp and hydrated so Delilah didn't complain about my dry skin again.

"Not just the women. I'm interested in everybody involved." He swallowed half his ale. "But let's start with the contestants. According to our information, there's Leesa, Daisy, Alyx with a 'y,' Bianca, Jackie, and Ashley."

"That's right. Bianca has a weird fake baby voice that she only uses with Sheridan." I snapped my fingers. "And she explicitly said she's not there to make friends."

"Hardly a confession. I think there's a difference between looking out for number one and murder."

I slumped against the back of my chair. "Ashley seems okay, although she's mentioned her personal journey twice already and that seems like two times too many."

He snorted with laughter.

"Jackie is certifiable and the crazy eyes don't help. She constantly looks like she's on the verge of replacing her eyeballs using a pair of tweezers."

"Now there's a visual. Anybody strike you as desperate enough to kill off the competition?"

"Bianca and Alyx strike me as hardcore."

He nodded. "I'll take a look at their backgrounds. Keep an eye on those two and let me know if you hear anything."

I saluted him. "Aye, aye."

"Notice any suspicious behavior by anyone else?"

"Kristoff has suspiciously bad taste in clothes. What makes him think a leprechaun should wear green from head to toe? It's like he's trying to camouflage himself."

"Deputy Bolan goes out of his way to never wear green."

"Smart man."

"I'll tell him you said so."

I smiled. "Please don't." The leprechaun and I had an interesting dynamic. Not quite the sibling rivalry that Bentley Smith and I had at *Vox Populi*, but similar.

"It's strange that women would come from all across the country to meet an absolute stranger. I guess the ones who live far away are willing to move."

"They could end up in a worse place than Starry Hollow." I would know.

"True. Who would you suggest we speak to after Bianca and Alyx?"

"Jackie, but only because of the repeated references to her mental state."

"Some men are attracted to crazy women. They get a thrill out of it."

"I don't get the sense Sheridan is that kind of guy. So far he seems kind of dull."

The sheriff laughed. "Only you would call a guy in the center of a dating show where a murder occurred dull."

"I mean, I can understand why they chose him. He's got that sort of bland attractiveness that appeals to certain women."

The sheriff shook his head. "Keep going, Rose. You're on a roll."

"I bet he has a baseball card collection."

"Is that indicative of a boring fella?"

I shrugged. "Only if he has time to alphabetize them."

"Remind me why you're wanting to date this guy again? Do you win money?"

I pretended to lock my lips and throw away the key. I noticed that his gaze lingered on my mouth and felt tiny jolts of electricity pulse through my body. Despite the surface-level conversation, the undertone was definitely more in the 'date' category. Even when we talked about murder, we managed to have a good time together. I'd have to make an effort not to enjoy my time with Granger Nash.

My phone pinged with an incoming text. I glanced at the unfamiliar number. *Hey, Ember. This is Daisy. Since we're not filming, some of us are getting together in honor of Tish if you want to hang out.*

The competitors were banding together in the wake of Tish's death? That was comforting.

Where and when? I typed back.

A club called Elixir at 9.

I'll be there. If nothing else, it would be an opportunity to get to know them better and dig for information.

"Anything good?" the sheriff prompted.

I tucked away my phone. "Good news. Looks like I can start spying for you sooner rather than later."

He looked slightly disappointed. "Do we at least get to finish our meal?"

"And here I thought you knew me."

The sheriff gazed at me with an expression of adoration that warmed me from the inside out. "Oh, I know you, Rose. And I know you'll eat every bite of your meal, one quarter of my meal, and then want dessert to wash it all down. Something chocolate. You would've had a second cocktail but the text update has spoiled your plan. You'll have one more drink with whoever texted you, though, and then call it a night."

"When did you become psychic?"

"I don't need to be psychic to know how you operate, Rose. You questioned how well I know you and I'm showing you."

Smiling, I raised my cocktail glass. "That you are. Cheers to knowing me and still sticking around."

He lifted his glass of ale and tapped it against mine. "Right back at you."

7

It was only when I arrived at Elixir that I realized the plans must have changed. There was a camera crew setting up inside and the women were nowhere to be seen. So much for female bonding.

I spotted a sultry werewolf just inside the entrance. "Hey, Deputy Pitt. I didn't expect to see you here."

The werewolf shrugged. "The producer called and asked me to be in charge of security tonight given the circumstances." Her gaze traveled around the interior of the club. There were glowing lava lights that threaded their way through the ceiling and floor. "Interesting choice for a backup venue."

Adrian stepped forward to greet us. "It's a great environment for the show. I'm so glad Daisy suggested it."

"What's the theme tonight?" I asked. I felt woefully unprepared.

"You'll all get gussied up in cocktail dresses and dance to the music. Sheridan assesses your movements. A lot of mating rituals in the animal world revolve around dance-type movements."

I glanced down at my shiny silver top and black pants. "I wish I'd had advanced warning. I thought production was shut down for now."

"Sorry, everything was done last minute. Delilah will find you a dress. The sheriff said we couldn't film at the crime scene, but he didn't say anything about not filming at all. As long as we don't leave town, we're good." Adrian cocked an eyebrow at Deputy Pitt. "Isn't that right, Deputy? You know, you could take Tish's place if you're interested. It wouldn't be against the rules to replace her."

"I like my current job better, thanks," Deputy Pitt replied.

"Adrian," a crew member called. "We need you."

Adrian excused himself and went to help.

Deputy Pitt regarded me. "When Granger said you were competing, I thought he was joking."

I folded my arms. "Gee, thanks."

"I'm not trying to insult you. I mean because of the two of you."

I perked up. "Why? What did he tell you?"

"Nothing specific." She gave me a lingering look. "You know, if you're putting yourself on the market for a guy like Sheridan Sinclair, then I don't see why I should behave myself."

I eyed her warily. "What's that supposed to mean?"

"It means Granger is fair game."

"He's your boss. Trust me, that's not an ideal combo."

She sniffed. "I'm a grown woman. I can determine that for myself."

"I'm a grown woman, but that doesn't mean I stop making mistakes. I have to imagine it's the same for you. Besides, between you and me, I'm not here to marry Sheridan."

The werewolf studied me. "Why not? Isn't handsome and wealthy the acceptable type for someone of your pedigree?"

Across the room, Kristoff snapped his fingers at me. "Stop flirting with the help and get into hair and makeup."

The deputy and I locked eyes and burst into laughter. "If he thinks this is flirting, heaven help this production," she said.

I hurried to the room they'd set up for the glam squad. There were mirrors and racks of dresses everywhere. Adrian wasn't kidding about the last-minute nature of the event.

The purple-haired fairy with the makeup brushes—Delilah—accosted me. "Your turn, sweetheart. Let's see. Dark hair. Light eyes. Pale as a vampire." She cast a glance over her shoulder. "Blue or purple dress!" She guided me to a chair in front of a mirror. "How well does your hair hold a curl?"

"Depends on how much you want to damage the ozone layer."

"Got it." She cupped her hands around her mouth and yelled, "Frizz control!"

Bottles and tools appeared. Before I knew it, I was surrounded by a team of fairies. They rubbed and powdered and slapped and tugged. I had no clue what was happening. I was like Cinderella in the scene where she transformed into her gown except I'd walk away with more bumps and bruises.

Delilah heaved an exasperated sigh. "Can somebody do something about those dark circles under her eyes?" She tapped my shoulder. "Do you have insomnia or something? You look like the walking dead."

Another fairy swooped in with a concealer stick and attacked the area under my eyes.

"Much better. Thanks, Tasha," the purple-haired fairy said.

"No problem." Tasha fluttered away to her next victim.

"Which dress?" a young satyr asked. He held a hanger in each hand—on the left was a blue dress that shimmered and on the right was a purple dress with a plunging neckline.

Delilah eyed the two choices. "What happened to the violet dress with the plunging neckline? That would be a great color for her."

The satyr tilted his head toward the main room. "Kristoff told me to give it to Ashley."

Delilah pursed her lips. "I guess she does have bigger boobs. Carry on."

"Shimmer," I said.

He tossed the dress at me and it landed on my lap.

"Do you have any idea how hard it is to move the whole set on a moment's notice?" the fairy complained. "Kristoff has no idea the amount of work that goes into each day of production. He just shows up and shouts."

"He hasn't been shouting as much as usual," the satyr commented. "I was wondering if he entered that anger management program that someone suggested."

Delilah snorted. "Highly doubtful. It's probably drugs."

"Enough chatter," Kristoff yelled. "We've already lost enough time."

I entered the main room just as Kristoff stood on a bar stool to address the group.

"Before we start filming, I'd like to have a moment of silence in honor of Tish," Kristoff began.

Everyone bowed their heads and the club fell silent. I'd been hoping they'd say a few words instead, to give me a better sense of the deceased woman, but no such luck.

Kristoff clapped his hands. "Great. Now, let's get moving. By the end of the night, one of you lucky ladies will have won a date night with Sheridan."

Excited murmurs followed the announcement. If I wanted to win the first date night, I was going to have to put on my boogie shoes.

To my great delight, the music was right up my alley. The other women didn't seem to know how to dance to 80s music, but thanks to my dad, I'd danced to enough songs by The Cure, George Michael, Prince, and Cyndi Lauper to make me a bonfire expert. A few contestants started copying my moves, which struck me as hilarious. I was neither a trendsetter nor a sheep. I marched to the beat of my own drum and I had a feeling it was going to serve me well tonight.

The music finally stopped and everyone rushed to the bar for drinks. As I walked across the room, I noticed Sheriff Nash standing beside Deputy Pitt. I waved and his jaw dropped when he realized it was me. Admittedly, it was a nice boost for my ego.

Flutes of champagne were handed out and everyone toasted to Sheridan and then to Tish's memory. The whole affair felt more like unnatural selection. Kristoff gave a speech about mating and reproduction which seemed like it would've been more at home at a zoo, not that this current environment was too far off.

When he finished, Ashley pressed her palm flat against her chest. "Thank you for the fine speech, Kristoff. I feel in my heart that this moment in time is crucial to my journey."

A groan escaped me and I quickly covered my mouth.

Leesa snickered.

Adrian produced a stuffed giraffe and tossed the toy to Sheridan.

"Time to choose the companion for your first official date," Kristoff announced. "And also, sadly, time to choose someone to go home."

Sheridan tucked the giraffe under his arm. "Ladies, any last words before I choose?"

Jackie emerged from the shadows in a body-hugging red dress that stopped just shy of revealing the color of her underpants, assuming she was wearing any. I swore she'd hiked up the dress a few inches since we were on the dance floor.

She placed a hand on her hip. "I'm *a lot* of personality, Sheridan Sinclair. I don't know if you have the stones to handle me."

Sheridan chuckled awkwardly, seemingly taken aback by her declaration. The other women wore matching expressions of disapproval.

"She's an envelope that got licked and slapped with a crazy stamp," Leesa whispered.

Yes, but was she crazy enough to kill?

"If no one else has anything to add, I've made my decision," Sheridan said.

The women fidgeted with excitement.

"Since tonight's topic was reproduction, this was an easy one. Ember's already shown she can reproduce. My date night will be with her."

"The *mom*?" Jackie asked, horrified.

Sheridan tossed a stuffed giraffe in my direction and I managed to catch the toy before it landed on the floor. I was half tempted to spike it like a football in the end zone. Dozens of dagger eyes pricked my skin as the other women realized they'd either not be chosen for one-on-one time or they had one more competitor to fend off.

At least my client would be pleased by the news.

"Well done," Daisy whispered.

"Thanks." I smiled and tried to look dreamy-eyed, although I probably looked more like I'd swallowed too much nighttime cold medicine.

"And now for the part of the evening I've been dreading." Sheridan rubbed the back of his neck. "One of you wonderful women has to go home."

"Not technically," I murmured. The sheriff wouldn't let anybody leave town until the murder was solved.

The air crackled with tension. I found myself eagerly anticipating Sheridan's decision on which contestant to let go. My money was on crazy Jackie.

His gaze swept the room and settled on the vampire. "Bianca, I'm sorry. You have not been selected."

Multiple pairs of shoulders relaxed and I heard soft sighs of relief. Only Bianca stood rigid. Her hot pink dress clung to her body like super glue. Her face contorted and I realized she was trying not to cry.

Sheridan urged her forward. "Time to part ways."

Bianca seemed to unstick her feet from the floor and walked toward him. "You're making a mistake," she seethed, abandoning her baby voice.

"I'm sorry you feel that way." Sheridan pecked her cheek and Adrian waved a flag offset and encouraged her toward them.

The vampire cast a parting glance over her shoulder at me. "You'll be next. He's only choosing you first so he doesn't look bad to all the mothers in the audience." She stalked offset and blew past Adrian, disappearing from view.

Once the cameras got their reaction shots, the production team called it a night. The bright lights turned off and it took me a moment to recover my eyesight. When I finally was able to focus, the sheriff was in front of me.

"Rose, I am speechless. Truly." He took a step back to admire me again. "You are a vision. I don't care what that nasty woman said, if that man doesn't choose you right now and end the competition, then he's missing more brain cells than a scarecrow."

I curtsied. "You're too kind."

"Care to take that dress out on the town or do you have to give it back first?"

I laughed. "We just ate together a few hours ago."

"I'm a werewolf. I'm always hungry."

I lowered my voice. "I'm not sure I should be fraternizing with any other men in view of Sheridan."

He hooked his thumbs through imaginary suspenders. "I'm the sheriff. It's your civic duty to keep me company while I eat tacos."

I laughed. "Tacos? You'd take me for tacos in this dress? Never mind."

He grinned. "Thought you were a big fan of tacos."

"Oh, I am, but this dress deserves fancier fare."

"I'm sure your aunt has a can of Fancy Feast squirreled away somewhere in the house for that cat of hers."

"Precious."

Deputy Pitt stepped forward and looped an arm through his. "He is, isn't he?"

"No, Precious is the name of my aunt's cat."

I noticed the sheriff pat her hand gently before removing his arm. She could peddle all she wanted, but Granger Nash wasn't interested in her wares, curvaceous and appealing though they may be. And here I thought she and I might be friends. At least I had Linnea and Aster. Still, it would be nice to befriend a woman in my age range who wasn't related to me.

"You should stick around here, Pitt," he said. "It's a good

opportunity to observe the suspects in their natural habitat."

I grunted. "I'm not sure this is anyone's natural habitat."

"I don't know about that." He motioned to the adjacent room where Alyx and Jackie were now dancing on the bar. Their dresses were short enough to see the color of their thongs. I averted my gaze. I'd witnessed enough unpleasantness for one day. One week, really.

"Let's go," I said. "One drink and then you can take me home."

"Such an enticing offer." He leaned closer. "And you can tell me if you learned anything noteworthy tonight."

We made it as far as the parking lot when my phone rang. "Excuse me one second." I turned away and whispered, "Hey, Mrs. Sinclair. How are you?"

"Geriatric and wealthy. I'd like an update for all the money I'm paying you."

Technically, she'd only paid me a deposit but it seemed unprofessional to quibble. "Good. I made it through to the next round and I have a one-on-one with Sheridan tomorrow night."

"That *is* good. Unfortunate news about the girl though."

"You heard about that?" I thought the production team was keeping a lid on it. I knew Florian was desperate to do the same. A murder was bad for everyone.

"Sheridan mentioned it when I spoke to him. I'm afraid he hasn't mentioned you specifically, which I took as a bad sign, but perhaps I was too hasty. I'd caution you to make an impression, my dear, before some trollop swoops in and steals him out from under you."

With some of these women, I wouldn't put it past them to do that literally. "I'll do my best, ma'am." I dropped the phone into my purse and turned to smile at the sheriff.

"Where would you like to go for an update?" Part of me hoped he said his place, but I couldn't bring myself to make the suggestion. What if he turned me down? After what happened between us before, I wouldn't blame him. I'd reject me, too.

"How about Wishing Well? I'm sure you have better things to do than spend half your day with me. We'll have a quick drink and call it a night."

I swallowed my disappointment and forced a smile. "Perfect."

8

The next morning I awoke feeling smug. I'd won the first date. Take that, witches! Okay, I was the only witch competing but still.

I stretched and took the obligatory walk with PP3. I meandered over to Marley's herb garden to check on the plants. She wanted me to talk to them whenever I was outside because apparently that helped them grow. Part of me was sure she'd hidden a camera in the fence and had made up the story to record me looking ridiculous. Then again, I was accustomed to looking ridiculous. It didn't tend to bother me.

I crouched in front of the first row of plants. "How you doin'?" I asked, using my best Joey from *Friends* voice.

PP3 barked at the row. The Yorkie was doing his part for the environment. Of course I also had to stop him from peeing on the plants. He was the cutest dog in the world, but not necessarily the smartest. At least he didn't try to eat them. Just because none of these were poisonous didn't mean they couldn't hurt his delicate stomach.

I pondered the plants for another beat. The killer had

used strychnine to poison Tish, which suggested they weren't a witch or wizard. That fit with the suspects' demographics. I was the only witch and the only wizard in the house was Florian.

"See you later, plants. It's time to get to work."

My date with Sheridan wasn't until later today. I wanted to tackle Marigold's case first. The sooner I tracked down Harold, the wayward elf, the sooner I got paid. The poor guy was probably on vacation and that was the only reason he didn't show up to mow Marigold's lawn. I'd clearly spent too much time pondering reproduction and mating rituals because the concept of Harold mowing Marigold's lawn had a dirty edge to it.

Earlier I'd instructed Marigold to send me Harold's address, which she'd dutifully provided. I scrolled through my text messages to find it.

"According to the map, it's 1.3 miles away," I told PP3. "I think I'll take my broomstick."

I'd hold off on a shower until right before my date with Sheridan. That way I didn't have to worry about the tangle of knots that flying was sure to produce. My ego wasn't huge, but it was big enough that I wanted to avoid looking like Bellatrix Lestrange on national television.

I flew along Coastline Drive, inhaling deeply along the way. The air smelled crisp and clean like freshly laundered sheets. I cast an admiring glance at the ocean waves as they rolled to shore. Balefire Beach was one of my favorite spots in town.

I had a near-miss with a seagull, but the bird wisely got out of my way. I turned right at Enchanted Road and flew until I reached the residential section of the road. The buildings here were mostly apartments. I spotted Sunny Gardens, which sounded more like a retirement home than an apartment complex, and came in for a landing.

In the dimly lit lobby, I found Harold's buzzer and pressed. Sunny Gardens was not living up to its name. So far it was neither sunny nor in possession of gardens.

The intercom crackled. "Who is it?"

"I'm looking for Harold."

"He isn't here." The voice was male, maybe late teens or early twenties.

"Any idea where I can find him?"

There was a pause. "No."

"Can I talk to you instead? I have cookies." To be fair, the cookies were still in my purse from yesterday. I'd stashed them in a zippered sandwich bag in case of an emergency.

"What kind of cookies?"

"I hope you like chocolate chip."

"Who doesn't like chocolate chip?"

The door buzzed open and I hurried through before he changed his mind. I easily located 3A and saw the door was already ajar.

"Hello?" I nudged open the door with my shoulder. "The cookie lady is here." I cringed at my own words. When did I become ninety?

An elf emerged from a narrow hallway. His blond hair was unkempt and his shirt and pants were rumpled as though he'd slept in his clothes. I was right about the age. He didn't look an hour older than twenty.

"I'm Ember and I come bearing gifts." I held up the zippered bag.

"I'm Timmy."

"Are you Harold's roommate?"

He nodded. "Why are you looking for him?"

"My client said he's missing and asked me to find him." I

unzipped the bag and set it on the coffee table between us. "Any idea where he is?"

Timmy swiped a cookie from the bag and gobbled it up. "I haven't had a chocolate chip cookie in years. My grandma used to bake them all the time." He took a moment to savor the taste. "That was awesome."

"Thanks. My daughter deserves the credit. She's become quite the baker." And I licked the spoon *and* the bowl. It was a perfect pairing.

Timmy took a second cookie and bit it in half. "I haven't seen Harold in a couple days. I assumed he went to visit his folks."

"Where do they live?"

"Starlight Falls."

"He wouldn't tell you he was going out of town?"

Timmy shrugged. "We don't have that kind of relationship. He does his thing and I do mine, and we split the rent."

"He didn't tell his client he was going away. She was expecting him to mow the lawn."

"I don't know what to tell you." Timmy tried to smooth his unruly blond locks but to no avail. The pieces stuck straight up again.

"Do you happen to have contact information for his parents?" I hated to worry them unnecessarily if Harold wasn't there, but I had to know.

"I think so. Hold on." He pulled his phone from his back pocket.

"Have you ever heard of Myrtle the Turtle Soup Lady?"

He gave me a blank look. "No. Who's that?"

I shook my head. "Forget it."

Timmy showed me his screen with the parents' phone number and I added it to my phone.

"Have you noticed anything different about Harold

lately? Anything to suggest he might take off for a few days to see his parents or blow off steam?" They might not be close buddies, but they still lived together. Timmy was likely to notice if Harold was acting out of character.

"Not really. We ordered takeout together last week and he seemed fine. He complained about how much work he had lined up, but that's not unusual." He lit up. "He did leave his phone here, though. That's weird, right? I don't know anyone who goes away without their phone."

No one Harold's age, that was for sure. "Can I see it?"

Timmy scurried to the hallway and returned a minute later with a phone. "Battery's dead now." He handed me a charger.

"Thanks." I pulled a business card from my purse and gave it to him. "If you think of anything else, will you let me know?"

He studied the card. "What does R&R stand for? Are you a railroad company?"

"Yes, a railroad company is interested in finding Harold."

My sarcasm was lost on the elf. "Cool. I like trains. Can you be interested in me?"

"It was nice to meet you, Timmy." I left the apartment no more knowledgeable than when I arrived. I hated to call Harold's parents, but it was the next logical step. If Harold was there, mystery solved.

I picked up the broomstick where I'd left it in the lobby and headed outside to make the call.

A woman picked up on the first ring. "Hello?"

"Hi, I'm looking for Harold. Is he there?"

"Harold? No, dear. He hasn't lived here in a couple years. May I ask who's calling?"

"I'm Penelope," I said, adopting my best version of a teen girl voice. "He and I went to school together, although he was a couple years ahead of me. I'm in town visiting my parents and I was hoping to get together."

"Oh, that's so nice. Unfortunately, he lives in Starry Hollow now. We haven't heard from him in about a week. If you manage to catch him, let him know his mother is thinking about him."

My chest tightened. Would Marley someday be too busy with her own life to remember to call me? I hoped not.

"I absolutely will. Thanks." I hung up. Another dead end. It looked like it was time to pursue the Myrtle and her infamous soup angle and I knew just the paranormal to ask.

HAVERFORD HOUSE WAS LOCATED on the outskirts of town in a secluded wooded area at the end of a long dirt lane flanked by enormous live oaks. It had been intimidating the first time I came here, but now it was like a second home to me.

I parked the car outside the red brick façade. The house was perfectly symmetrical with two large windows on either side of the portico and three same-sized windows on the second floor. A widow's walk adorned the rooftop. Moss and ivy had taken over much of the building and a large weeping willow kissed the left side of the house. The rusty gate of the wrought-iron fence hung askew, and I wondered why Jefferson never got around to fixing it. The ghostly manservant was probably too busy tending to his mistress's interior needs to worry about the exterior.

I entered the house to find Artemis Haverford on the settee in her parlor room, balancing a saucer and teacup on her bony thigh. I wouldn't have attempted that without a bit more cushion, but Artemis lived in her own world and did as she pleased. Although we were members of the same coven, she didn't attend meetings nor did she kiss my aunt's derriere, which was probably one of the reasons we got along so well. Whereas I aggressively didn't care about the opinions of others, Artemis gently and quietly gave zero ducks. Same outcome, different method.

"How's our sweet Marley?" the elderly witch asked. She adjusted the lace collar of her white dress. Artemis looked like she'd stepped out of the pages of *Grey Gardens Quarterly*.

"Good. She's been hanging around with a new friend I haven't met yet. Some witch called Jinx."

"That's nice that she's making new friends. Is there a problem with Jinx?"

Artemis was more perceptive than she appeared. "No problem. It's just that we seemed to go from no mentions of Jinx to twenty mentions of her per day."

"And you don't trust it."

"I don't know if trust is the right word. It puts me on my guard, that's all. Any relationship that takes you by storm, whether it be a friendship or a romance, needs to be given a serious case of side-eye."

Artemis peeled her lips from her tea-stained teeth. "That's being a protective mama bear. Every child should be so fortunate."

"Granger would say I'm more of a broomstick mama, hovering too close." He'd even bought me a T-shirt with the logo.

"Nonsense. There's a difference between protective and controlling, as you well know." She paused to take a dainty sip of tea. "Speaking of which, how is Hyacinth?"

I started to cough. That was the shadiest segue Artemis had ever uttered and I was here for it. "She's out of town, thank goodness."

"I was wondering how she was coping with all the drama at Thornhold. Now I understand. Who steered this ship into an iceberg? Florian?"

I laughed. "He didn't commit the actual murder, but he's responsible for everything else."

The witch clucked her tongue. "Poor woman. Does the sheriff know what happened yet?"

"Not yet. Where did you hear about it?"

She tapped the side of her teacup, thinking. "We were at the Wish Market, weren't we, Jefferson?" She raised her voice at the end to be heard by her ghostly manservant.

The air chilled and I knew Jefferson had entered the chat. A fresh cup of tea floated toward me on a tray.

"I guess it doesn't matter who told you," I said. "It's just that the sheriff is trying to keep it quiet for the town's sake."

"And yours, I imagine. If Hyacinth finds out and knows you were involved, that will only make matters worse between you."

She was right. My aunt might overlook Florian's role in order to focus on me.

"We know it was poison, but that's about it."

Artemis's pale face regained a bit of color. "Poison? Do tell. What kind?"

"Nothing magical. Strychnine."

"How fascinating. Method of delivery?"

"Don't know yet. There was no evidence of a drink or anything to suggest she ingested it." I made a noise at the back of my throat. "While we're on the subject of fascinating crimes, are you familiar with someone called Myrtle the Turtle Soup Lady?"

"Not that name explicitly, but there's a Myrtle who lives out by the Whitethorn. It's a small cottage by the sea. A charming place."

"Is she a witch?"

Artemis wet her chapped lips. "No, I don't believe so. I think she might be a fairy, but I honestly don't recall."

That made sense. A witch would be on the coven's radar. A reclusive fairy like Myrtle, on the other hand, could escape their notice.

"Why do you ask?"

"Marigold hired me to find someone she thinks might have been taken by Myrtle for the purpose of making soup."

Artemis jutted out her lower lip. "A Hansel and Gretel-style witch at work. Interesting. I'm afraid I don't know her."

If Artemis didn't know her, I couldn't imagine who would. She was a staple of the Starry Hollow community and had been around for centuries.

"No worries, thanks. I'll keep digging." I swirled the milk around in my cup with the small spoon and watched the dark brown fade to a pale beige.

"Tell me more about this show. I'm intrigued. Are you truly courting this gentleman on national television?"

Courting was a polite way of describing it.

"I'm vying for his affection, along with a handful of other women."

"I suppose that's one way to land a husband." Her brow wrinkled. "I didn't get the sense you were that desperate, Ember."

"I'm not, but I can't say more than that."

She nodded. "I understand. You don't need to elaborate."

Artemis might be old and in love with the past, but she never failed to understand me even when she had to read between the lines. It was a rare gift and one I appreciated.

"I won the first date with Sheridan—that's his name. That gives me a leg up over the other women."

"That's excellent and not at all surprising."

"You wouldn't say that if you saw the other women."

"Beauties, huh?"

"Beautiful. Determined. Cutthroat."

She finished her tea and set the cup and saucer on the end table. "If anyone can best them, it's you. Where will you go on your date?"

"According to the text from the producer, I'm supposed to meet him at Balefire Beach."

"Maybe you're to take a surfing lesson together."

I groaned. "That would be...not ideal." I sighed. "I think the production team likes the element of surprise."

"Well, they certainly got that with a dead contestant. I can't imagine anyone was expecting that result."

"Definitely not." A thought occurred to me. "You know what? We're in need of a house until Thornhold is cleared for production. What would you think about having your house featured on television?"

"Will all those hormonal women have to stay here?"

"Probably, but maybe we can persuade Kristoff to only film during the day and then have the cast and crew stay in a hotel at night."

Artemis appeared thoughtful. "Allow me to consult the tiles." She pulled a pouch of Scrabble letters from the side of the sofa cushion and shook the bag. She scattered the tiles across the coffee table and flipped over five of them. Y-E-S-N-O.

I laughed. "That's as clear as mud."

"Is there a chance someone might get arrested while you film here?"

I grimaced. "Yes. Is that a dealbreaker?"

She slapped her thigh. "Are you kidding? Tell them the doors of Haverford House are open for business."

9

Marley ambled into my bedroom with the gait of a foal. She was growing up right in front of my eyes. Sometimes the realization took my breath away.

"I can't believe you got the first one-on-one with Sheraton."

I gave her a pointed look. "He's not a hotel chain. His name is Sheridan. And I have you to thank for the honor."

She frowned. "Me? Why?"

"The fact that I can reproduce bodes well for the survival of the species, apparently."

Fits of laughter exploded from her. "This show is so dumb. I can't believe you're doing it."

"Mama's got to pay the bills."

"You're a private investigator now. Can't you investigate something?"

"I'm working on a job for Marigold. And the murder, too. The sheriff wants to have someone on the inside."

She smirked. "And how does he feel about your special time with a complete stranger?"

I looped earrings through my lobes. "You remember this is for work, right?"

"Who do you think killed...what was her name again?"

"Tish and I have no idea. I'll see what I can find out from Sheridan." While also keeping him interested enough not to choose some other woman and giving his grandmother a heart attack. Two birds with one bimbo.

"Aren't you worried?"

I cut a sideways look at her. "Oh, honey. It's not as though I'm interested in him."

"I don't mean that. Aren't you worried you'll become a target? If the killer wants to win and they think you're in the lead..."

"What's their plan? Kill every woman until she's the last one standing? It'll be pretty obvious who the killer is by then." I patted her cheek. "I'm not worried. If someone tries to off me, I'll go Jersey on their butt."

Marley snickered. "Wouldn't it be better to go One True Witch?"

I shook my head. "Not as powerful."

"Good luck, Mom. Sherbert's going to love you."

"As long as he loves me until filming ends, that's all I care about. Make sure to do your homework while I'm gone. I'll be back well before bedtime."

"Okay. What's for dinner?"

"There are leftovers in the fridge."

I drove to the beach and was relieved I'd chosen comfortable shorts and shoes because it appeared our date involved body bubbles. I vacated the car and joined the crew on the sand where Sheridan was already wrapped in an enormous blue bubble.

"She's here," someone yelled.

"Hurry," Delilah said, flying over to me. "We need to get

you in a bubble before we lose the light." She craned her neck and screamed, "Purple!"

"What's going on? How are we supposed to conduct a date if we're ensconced in inflatable body armor?"

Delilah chuckled. "You think any of these dates are meant to be real? If it doesn't entertain, it doesn't belong on television. Be thankful you're not making plaster casts of your breasts today."

I glanced at my chest. "Would it have been with the support of a bra or without?"

Two crew members ran toward me, rolling a giant purple bubble between them.

"We won't be reproducing in that," I remarked.

Delilah snorted. "Wouldn't stop some of these women from trying."

The crew members helped me into the inflatable bubble and backed away. I now resembled an oversized grape.

"Now what?" I asked.

"Have fun," Delilah advised and fluttered away.

"Glad you could make it, Ember." Sheridan tried to make his way toward me, but he kept rolling backward.

I made an effort to maneuver toward him. For an object the same shape as a wheel, the bubble proved challenging to move. When we finally reached each other, we underestimated the distance and bounced off each other's surfaces. The entire crew exploded with laughter.

"This is ratings gold," Adrian said.

"What kind of date is this supposed to be?" I asked. There was no way to act sexy in the middle of a giant purple bubble, not that I'd mastered the art of seduction anyway. The other women were fortunate they didn't land the first date. I couldn't imagine Alyx or Leesa being pleased to look like the Stay Puft Marshmallow Man when they're trying to make a good impression.

"I'd say just roll with it," Sheridan began, "but I don't seem capable of rolling in the right direction."

"What does this date have to do with survival of the fittest?" I grumbled.

"This part? Nothing. The point is to make a mockery of us. Helps the viewers relate to us more."

As hard as I tried, I couldn't push the bubble closer to him. I kept sinking into the sand, which made it difficult to maneuver the bubble. If I didn't figure out a workaround, the entire date would be spent like two grapes at opposite ends of the same vine. I decided to pull an ace out of my sleeve.

Channeling my inner witch, I said, "Bullae, ausculto." The bubble around me seemed to soften. I focused my will on Sheridan's bubble and uttered the same words.

"What did you say? My Latin's a little rusty."

Easier to show him. "Bubble, move forward two feet," I commanded.

The bubble bounced forward two feet, causing sand to spray in all directions.

"Awesome," Sheridan said, his eyes shining with pleasure.

"Now you try."

He lit up. "Really?"

"I used magic on both of them. You should be able to command your bubble, too."

His expression was pure joy, like a kid who got exactly the gift he wanted for Christmas. "Bubble, two feet to the right on a diagonal."

His bubble bounced and shifted so that we were facing each other.

"Hi," he said, grinning.

"What now?"

"No clue. I thought you might know. Isn't this the type of activity you do with your daughter?"

I laughed. "Not even close. Marley is more into books."

"A reader, huh? Who's her favorite author?"

I resisted the urge to name Alec Hale, although it was probably true. "You'd have to ask her. Do you like to read?"

"I do. Does that surprise you?"

"Too soon to tell. What kind of books do you like?"

"Nonfiction for the most part, although I like the occasional murder mystery. Only when the detective is a dude, though. I can't relate to any of those lady detectives." He paused. "Our kids would be readers then, huh?"

"Not necessarily. I don't think genes are that straightforward."

"Books aren't a dealbreaker for me, although I'd like a son with physical skills. Someone who excelled in sports."

Of course he would.

"What if that didn't happen?" I asked. I knew it was risky to challenge his perceptions on our date, but I was genuinely interested to hear his answers.

"What if I don't have a son?" He shrugged. "I'm sure I can relate to a girl."

"No, I mean what if you have a son, but he's not good at sports? What if he loves insects and dinosaurs and trips over his own two feet?"

Sheridan blinked. "Is this your way of telling me you're clumsy? You're supposed to be selling yourself on this date, you know. That's the point."

I sucked in a breath and prayed for patience. "This isn't about me, Sheridan. I'm curious how you would handle not having your expectations met." For the first time ever, it seemed.

"If he's not good, I'll hire a personal coach. I have the money. Why not use it for a worthy cause?"

Internally, I was screaming. Either Sheridan didn't get it or he didn't want to get it. "I think one of the best things we can do for our kids is not burden them with our expectations."

He grunted. "You don't want your kid to amount to anything? That's not very parental of you."

"That's not what I'm saying. I mean it's best to let our kids simply be who they are without carrying the weight of our expectations. Ever hear of unconditional love? Kids know when they're accepted as they are." I paused. "And they also know when they're not. At the end of the day, I just want my child to be happy."

His expression softened. "Yeah, I guess I see your point. So your daughter isn't athletic but she likes to read. What else?"

"She's musical. She loves animals. She's great with plants."

"Plants," Sheridan repeated, slightly dumbfounded.

"Enough with the talking heads! More bouncing, please!" Adrian's voice echoed across the field.

Sheridan and I automatically started bouncing side by side away from the cameras. Let them catch up.

"What do you think of the other women so far?" I asked. Now seemed like a good time to dig for information.

"Jackie seems nuts. Leesa makes me laugh. Daisy and I only live a few miles apart, which is cool. Alyx is beautiful but the 'y' in her name is a bit extra."

"Why'd you choose Bianca to go home?"

He smiled. "Don't you want to keep the focus on you? This is your big chance."

He was right, and now I felt torn between my duty to my client and my promise to the sheriff. I'd have to try my best to balance both needs.

"Isn't it hard to look at your dating options without wondering which one might be capable of murder?"

His brow furrowed. "Yeah, it's awful what happened to Tish."

"Change the subject," Adrian shouted.

"That's what editors are for," I mumbled.

"How much magic can you do?" Sheridan asked, bowing to the pressure.

I tried to encapsulate my answer in a single sentence but failed. "How much time do you have?"

"Well, these dates can last as long as I want. Even overnight." He winked.

Not in this lifetime, buddy. "I didn't know I had magic until I moved to Starry Hollow. I thought I was a regular human."

"Wow. That's so cool. I always wanted magic. Instead I had a family of inventors. Problem is I suck at inventions, much to their disappointment. Well, except my grandmother. She thinks I'm meant for greater things." He gave a rueful shake of his head. "I guess I understand what you mean about knowing when your family doesn't accept you for who you are, though."

"It doesn't feel good, does it?"

He seemed to contemplate the question. "No, it doesn't."

"What kind of things have they invented?" I pictured a mansion filled with robot butlers and mechanical dogs that fetched toys.

He pushed against the inside of his bubble and rolled

forward. "Where to start? A retractable lamp that's as tall or short as you need. An aqua-based treadmill that allows you to walk on water. Great exercise for the legs. It's one of the reasons my family is loaded. They've sold off a few of the better ones and made a mint."

"That's pretty awesome. I don't know why you think magic is the superior option."

"Are you kidding? Magic is so much better than a lamp. There's no science behind it. No labor. You just do it. I was always so jealous of the wizards in school. They got all the girls with their potions and spells. Nymphs have to find other ways to get attention."

"I'm sure you had your share of admirers." He was handsome and wealthy. There was no way girls weren't fighting for his attention.

"I dated, but no one seriously. My family made sure of that."

My eyebrows inched up. "Your family meddled in your personal relationships? Sounds familiar." Of course, his family's willingness to meddle was the entire reason I was standing in a purple bubble right now.

"You, too?"

Bounce. Bounce. We headed toward the water.

I nodded. "My aunt thinks because she has more money than Zeus that she can control everyone in her orbit."

His head bobbed. "My grandmother is the same. She's constantly trying to dictate my choices. It's infuriating. Sometimes I fantasize about running away and changing my name."

"What stops you?"

His head dipped. "I'm ashamed to admit it, but I'd make a terrible pauper."

Magic & Marriage

The money was important to him. Fair enough. Nobody wanted to be poor if they could avoid it.

"Have you tried telling her to butt out?"

He barked a short laugh. "Have you tried that with your aunt?"

"Yes."

"And how'd that work out for you?"

I exhaled. "Not well. I lost my job and my boyfriend."

He whistled. "But did she cut you off financially?"

"She wasn't supporting me so that didn't matter. But she owned the weekly paper where I worked and made sure to twist the knife. I didn't have a lot of money to begin with, so it wasn't as though I was accustomed to a luxurious lifestyle."

Sheridan's gaze softened. "I am, and I guess I don't want to lose it. It's part of my identity. I'd do anything to keep it."

I smiled. "Not anything. You're here, right? What if she doesn't approve of your choice?"

"It'll be too hard for her to stop me. She won't want to look bad in the eye of the public. Our family image is too important to her. When I leave this show, she'll be forced to accept my future wife."

"Is that why you decided to do the show?"

He met my gaze. "Yeah, it is. I needed a way out from under her iron thumb. Everyone says Kristoff is a tyrant, but that's because they haven't met my grandmother. She stopped by to see me the other day and the crew felt like they couldn't make eye contact with her. I told them if they see her near the set again to block her. She'll only try to push her agenda."

He had no idea.

"So you've traded one dictator for another."

He smiled. "Yeah, but this thing with Kristoff is only temporary. And once I have my bride, I'll be home-free."

I moved to offer his hand a sympathetic pat and ended up smacking the inside of the bubble. "I hope it works out for you, Sheridan." I felt a twinge of guilt for my subterfuge. I understood his predicament in a way that few others could. If it weren't for the murder, I might even be tempted to return Mrs. Sinclair's deposit and call off the arrangement, but since I was here anyway…

We bounced our bubbles into the surf and started to float. A wave came along and pushed us back to shore.

"I want to get to know you," Sheridan said. "You're a hard person to read. Tell me what you're looking for in a man."

I didn't love the change in focus to me, but it was inevitable under the circumstances.

"You think I'm hard to read? That's funny. I usually feel like if you want to know what I'm thinking, you just have to look at my face."

He shook his head. "Not to me. Right now all I've got is attractive and confident—and pretty darn magical."

It wasn't terrible to hear someone describe me in those terms.

I was surprised to hear myself answering honestly. "I want what most women want, I think. Honesty. Emotional maturity. Communication." I thought of Alec and his failure to tick any one of those boxes. No wonder it didn't work out. I'd been forcing myself to accept less than my bare minimum.

"How long ago did you get divorced?" Sheridan asked.

I offered a sad smile. "Not divorced. Widowed."

"Oh, I didn't realize. I'm sorry to hear that. That's really sad." He seemed genuinely moved.

"It happened a long time ago. Marley's the best daughter a mom could ask for, so I got lucky there."

"Any relationships since then?"

"None that resulted in marriage." I didn't want to talk about my recent romantic history. I had too many emotions bubbling under the surface—emotions that I'd been steadfastly trying to work through during moments of quiet self-reflection. I wasn't about to discuss them on television.

The camera crew caught up to us and Adrian scolded us for moving out of view.

"You're wired for sound, but the video will be terrible," he moaned.

"You should've told us what to expect," I said. "Maybe given us a couple of pointers."

Sheridan nodded. "Ember's right. If it weren't for her magic, we'd be stuck in awkward mode." He glanced around at his blue bubble. "Well, I guess it's still pretty awkward." He grinned at me. "But you made me forget I look like an idiot. Believe me. That's not easy to do." He struggled to get out of the bubble. "How am I supposed to kiss her if I'm contained in this stupid thing?"

"We don't have to kiss on the first date," I said. "There's something endearing about waiting for the right moment." I knew it was risky though. The women seemed to view kisses as currency to spend and I was volunteering to be broke.

"Old-fashioned," Sheridan said, nodding his approval. "I wouldn't have guessed that being a teen mom and all, but I guess once bitten, twice shy."

Ouch.

Despite brief flashes of humanity, Sheridan wasn't really my type, not that I was surprised. My type would never appear on television to find his future bride. My type would wait patiently and not pass judgment on me. My type was polite and charming and selfless.

I stopped the runaway train of thought because I knew exactly where it would lead and I wasn't in the right frame of mind to go there. I blocked all thoughts of him. Right now I was in the midst of a date that I needed to go well. Sheridan wasn't stupid. He might sense that I was preoccupied with thoughts of someone else.

"I had a good time with you, Ember. Thanks for rocking and rolling with me." He laughed at his own joke. Then he made the mistake of rolling toward me in an effort to kiss me. Our bubbles bounced off each other again and rolled away.

"Libero," I said.

The bubbles broke in half and landed on the sand around us.

Sheridan stared at the pieces in awe. "It would be so awesome to have a kid with magic."

I smiled. "It's pretty amazing. I can't argue with that. Have a good night, Sheridan."

"That's it? She's leaving?" I heard Adrian say to no one in particular. He sounded annoyed by the outcome.

As Florian would say, always leave them wanting more.

I simply stepped over the rubble and walked away.

10

With the first date under my belt, I felt better about my chances of winning the competition. I wasn't a particularly competitive person, but I was stubborn about completing the job I was hired to do. If that meant snagging the final giraffe, then so be it. My confidence increased when Kristoff texted the next morning to congratulate me on appealing to Sheridan on an emotional level during our outing. The executive producer seemed to think I chose that angle deliberately rather than let it unfold naturally. Was everyone that jaded?

Kristoff also said there'd be no filming today due to a snafu with the next location, which reminded me of Artemis's willingness to film in Haverford House. I sent a message to Florian to tell him. I'd let him work out the logistics with Kristoff and the rest of the production team. At least now I had a day to catch up on domestic duties. The pantry was looking painfully bare.

I drove into town to stock up on supplies. I eavesdropped on conversations in the store, but no one was talking about the murder. Maybe word hadn't spread as much as I'd believed. That was a relief. Aunt Hyacinth would cut her trip short if she found out her home had been tainted by both death and loose women. The horror!

As I walked back to the car with bags of groceries, I noticed a petite blonde standing outside Starry Hollow Realty. She was so intent on the listings posted in the window that she failed to register my presence even when I stood directly beside her.

"Leesa?"

Her body jolted and she turned to look at me. "Oh, hey. Emma, right? Or is it Emily? I always get those two names confused."

"It's Ember, actually." I inclined my head toward the listings. "Thinking about relocating here?"

She cut a glance at the window. "No, no. I just like to browse. I'm always interested to see how other real estate agents handle their listings. I also like to compare markets with mine."

"And how does Starry Hollow compare with your town?"

She bit her lip, thinking. "Well, for starters, this is a tourist town so your prices are higher. I can get a similar three-bedroom house in my town for one hundred thousand less."

"I could never have afforded my house here. I was fortunate enough to inherit it."

Leesa looked at me with renewed interest. "That's right. You live in a cottage right near Thornhold, don't you?"

I nodded. "Rose Cottage. It belonged to my parents. I was broke and unemployed when I moved here, so that house was a gift from the gods."

"I think you're really brave to compete as a single mom. I wouldn't have had the guts to do it."

"Do you think it's that big of a deal?"

Magic & Marriage

She laughed. "Are you serious? It's a huge deal. You're just lucky you live locally and didn't have to leave your kid behind to film the show."

"I wouldn't have done it otherwise." I also wouldn't have done it without being paid by a client, but Leesa didn't need to know that. "I guess you don't have any children at home."

Leesa grimaced. "Absolutely not. Jake and I don't want kids. It's the one thing we agree on." As soon as the words left her mouth, her face morphed into a ripe tomato. "I mean, I don't...Sheridan doesn't..."

Except Sheridan very much did. In fact, he'd made it clear his future progeny were of the utmost importance to him.

I couldn't let the moment slide. "Who's Jake?"

She struggled for a moment but finally blew out a defeated breath. "Oh, screw it. Confession time. I live with a long-term boyfriend at home, okay? His name is Jake and he's a musician."

"You have a long-term boyfriend?"

A puff of air formed a circle on the window and she wiped it away with her sleeve. "I do. We'd like to get married next year if we can afford it."

"Why be here if you don't want to marry Sheridan?"

She shrugged unapologetically. "Because I want the money that comes with the exposure."

"There's no money at stake."

"Not directly, but you know how it goes. Some of the previous contestants have gotten spokesperson agreements, sponsorship agreements. If you make the right impression on the show, it can be lucrative even if you don't win."

I clearly hadn't done my research. "You want to be a spokesperson?"

"I want a cash injection. I've been looking to expand my

business and that takes advertising, which isn't cheap. Plus the wedding." She lifted her chin. "I refuse to hold our reception in a fire hall. That might have been good enough for my parents, but not for me."

"What does Jake think about you on the show? Or did you not tell him?" If he didn't watch the show, it was possible he'd never find out.

"Oh, he knows. He's staying here in town, actually. I sneak off to see him whenever I can, which is how I ended up at this window." She jerked a thumb over her shoulder. "He's staying at an inn up the road."

"Palmetto Inn?"

She pointed at me. "That's the one. Do you know it?"

"My cousin Linnea owns it."

"She's lucky. It's a real pretty place."

"She's put a ton of work into it. The building is historic, so something always needs fixing."

Leesa smiled. "A fixer-upper. I bet Sheridan's never had to live in one of those. I spent most of my life in rundown buildings. I swore I'd never let myself fall back to that level."

"It might interest you to know that Thornhold is Linnea's childhood home."

Her eyebrows crept up her forehead. "You don't say?"

"She disappointed her mother by marrying the wrong guy." I shrugged. "So she ended up fending for herself." Although Linnea had slowly inched her way back into her mother's good graces.

Light sparked in Leesa's eyes. "I'm familiar with that scenario."

Leesa was being so forthcoming that I decided to steer the conversation toward another subject. "What are your thoughts on the Tish situation?"

Her face darkened. "A terrible tragedy."

"Any guesses as to what happened?"

She snorted. "You mean who killed her? No idea. The police still have me on their list. If that sheriff weren't so hot, I'd be annoyed by all the questions. I wish I could tell him the truth and be out of the crosshairs, though. It's hard to focus on the competition when I'm worried about being arrested."

I shot her a quizzical look. "Why can't you tell him the truth?"

"Why do you think? I was with Jake when Tish was killed. That's why I told the sheriff I was alone."

I balked. "Leesa, you need to confess this."

"I can't. They'll boot me from the show."

"You could end up arrested."

"Admitting the truth doesn't get me off the hook. I could still end up arrested."

"Do you remember what time you left Thornhold?"

"Not exactly, but it was right after filming ended because I promised Jake we'd eat together. Kristoff was handing out flutes of champagne, but I didn't bother to take one."

There was no way Leesa could have killed Tish. Strychnine would've worked quickly, which meant Tish would've died hours earlier if Leesa had administered it.

"Leesa, you have a solid alibi. Jake exonerates you."

Leesa didn't seem to care. "I'm willing to take the risk. I didn't do it, which means I won't be convicted. I only need to ride it out until the show wraps up production."

I gaped at her. "If you end up arrested, that will go on your record. Even if you get sponsorships or whatever, an arrest could void the contract."

"Like I said, it's a chance I'm willing to take in order to stay on the show."

I tried another tack. "You also realize if the police focus

on you as a suspect, that's attention being diverted from the real killer, right? The sheriff's department is pretty small here. Their resources are limited."

She tossed her blond hair over her shoulder in a haughty gesture. "If they do their job right, they'll figure out I'm lying."

"Leesa..."

She cut me off with a sharp glance. "And don't even think about telling the producers the truth. I never should've told you about Jake." She looked me up and down. "You said you're a witch. What did you do—use a truth spell on me?"

"I didn't use magic on you. You volunteered the information. I'm more concerned with finding Tish's killer than winning some stupid competition that reduces women to objects and brings out their worst qualities."

Her sculpted brows drew together. "If you don't want to win, then why compete? If Sheridan focuses on you as a bride, then that's attention being diverted from the rest of us." She folded her arms in a smug manner, appearing pleased to use my own words against me.

"I have an obligation to fulfill," I said vaguely. There was no way I'd tell her the truth. I wasn't only staying to satisfy Mrs. Sheridan, but to help the sheriff.

A small smile emerged. "It seems we both have our secrets. I suggest we agree to keep them." As she stepped closer to me, her smile faded and her face hardened. "If you breathe one word to Sheridan or the producers, I will make your life a living hell."

"Noted."

She practically snarled. "Promise me you won't tell them."

"I promise not to tell Sheridan or the producers."

Satisfied, Leesa turned on her heel and marched away.

I DUMPED my grocery bags in the car and headed straight to Palmetto Inn. I only promised I wouldn't tell Sheridan or the producer. I didn't say anything about Linnea or the sheriff. Although I was almost one hundred percent certain Leesa was truthful about her alibi, it would be easy enough to confirm her story before sharing the information with law enforcement.

I found Linnea alone in the kitchen. There seemed to be pots and pans on every square inch of counter space. Linnea's white-blond hair was fashioned in a messy bun and her 'Kitchen Witch' apron was dusted with flour and sugar.

"What's going on back here?" I asked.

She didn't smile. "A culinary disaster. I should have known better than to try this recipe without magic."

I approached the counter with caution. There was nowhere to touch that wouldn't involve leaving with traces of food on my black clothes.

"Why are you cooking without magic?"

"Because Rick suggested I'm not capable of it."

Frederick 'Rick' Simms was Linnea's minotaur boyfriend. "Why does he care whether or not you use magic in the kitchen?"

She tilted her head and sighed. "You know how non-magic users can be. They think we're overly reliant on our powers to accomplish basic tasks."

"But if you know that's not true, then why feel the need to prove it to him?"

She untied her apron and tossed it on the counter. "That's a good question and one I should probably explore with a therapist."

I pressed my lips together. "Linnea, is everything okay between you and Rick?"

"Yes, it's only a bump in the road. Nothing serious." She opened the refrigerator and pulled out a jug of iced tea. "How about a drink?"

"Sure."

She poured two tall glasses of iced tea and passed one to me. "How's Natural Selection?"

"Strange."

"Any leads on the murderer?"

"Granger and his team are working on it."

Linnea fixed me with a curious expression. "What do you think of the new member of his team?"

"Deputy Pitt? She's nice."

"And *very* pretty. I can see men committing crimes just to be arrested by her."

"That's one way to meet your future wife."

"No stranger than a television show." She sipped her iced tea. "What are the other women like? Are the claws out?"

"Oh, definitely. These women are committed." And some of them needed to *be* committed.

"Wyatt should be the prospective mate on a show like that. He'd be in his natural element."

"Except the point is to marry one of them. I don't think he'd be thrilled with that part."

"Yeah, I think once was enough for him. What do you think of the guy? What's his name again?"

"Sheridan Sinclair. He's...what you would expect."

She laughed. "Such effusive praise. I can practically hear the wedding bells."

"I don't know how anybody can truly get to know him. When his tongue will have been down five throats and his hand on three breasts in the course of a single day, how can he be expected to tell the women apart? Don't all those body parts start to seem the same?"

Linnea cocked her head. "Five tongues but only three breasts?"

"Some women want to take it slower." And women like me wanted to take it so slow we basically rolled backward in a purple body bubble. "Any word from your mother?"

Linnea drank her iced tea. "Not a peep. Don't worry, I already swore to Florian not to breathe a word about the show or the murder."

"What about Aster?"

"She's as worried as Florian. Don't forget she's on the tourism board, too. Mother will blame her as well."

I noticed dark circles under my cousin's eyes. Whatever was going on with Rick, it was costing her valuable sleep.

"Are you sure this thing with Rick is only a bump in the road?"

Linnea stared into her glass of iced tea. "I hope so. I think he's worried that my magic creeps into areas that he'd rather keep magic-free, if you know what I mean."

My brow lifted. "He's worried you're using magic in the bedroom?"

"In a way that might reflect poorly on his skills." She groaned. "He's a freaking minotaur. What could I possibly need magic for?"

"So you're trying to stop using magic for basic tasks to show him you don't rely on it."

"In a nutshell." Her gaze traveled around the messy kitchen. "But I'm so busy between this place, shuttling the kids to and from activities, and Rick that I would much rather use magic when I can so that I can enjoy my downtime."

"Of course. Who wouldn't?" I frowned. "Not that I want the details, but did something specific happen to make him believe there was magic involved during your...performance?"

Her cheeks turned pink. "We had an incredible night last week. The kids were each sleeping at a friend's house and I didn't have any guests at the inn so we had the whole place to ourselves. *That* was magical."

"Why would he think it was more than an amazing night?"

She closed her eyes. "We ended up on the floor afterward..."

"The floor? I'd end up with a backache and a kink in my neck. No wonder he thought there was magic involved."

She laughed. "He found my wand under the bed and assumed I'd used a spell. I tried to explain that it wasn't there on purpose and that leaving a wand lying around doesn't result in a spell, but he refused to listen."

"It sounds like he was already feeling insecure and seeing the wand fed into it." Although Linnea was right. Rick was the minotaur version of Adonis. He had nothing to worry about.

"I can't imagine what would make him insecure. I never noticed it before." She stopped talking and her eyes widened.

"What is it?"

Her expression turned to stone. "One word—Wyatt."

Of course. Only Wyatt Nash, Linnea's ex-husband, would have the necessary skills to make Rick feel uncomfortable.

"Have they seen each other recently?"

She nodded. "Wyatt came by to see the kids last week

when Rick was here. He made a big deal about finding his football in the master bedroom closet."

"And what? Rick thinks that Wyatt actually left it here recently?"

"I'm sure Wyatt gave him that impression. Wyatt also made a snide comment about me phoning in the relationship which was why he sought company outside the marital home. He said I could've at least had the decency to use magic to keep things interesting."

Typical Wyatt. "He got in Rick's head."

"And now Rick probably thinks I've started using magic because I'm bored with him." She slapped her forehead. "I swear to the gods, Wyatt needs to have his mouth sewn shut."

I smirked. "Might've helped with the extramarital company, too."

"I'm sure you didn't come here to talk about my relationship issues."

"No, but I'm always happy to listen. While I'm here, though, I need to check your guest list. Do you have a visitor by the name of Jake?"

Linnea tucked a loose strand of hair behind her ear. "Yes, Jake Davis. What's this about?"

"One of the contestants, Leesa. She says her boyfriend is staying here and that she was with him at the time of the murder. I'd like to verify her story."

She smiled. "You're not a reporter anymore, you know."

"This is for Granger. He asked me to be his woman on the inside."

She gave me a knowing look. "I bet he did."

"Stop. He asked me for professional reasons."

"Okay. I'll pretend along with you. Can you describe Leesa?"

"I can do better." I pulled out my phone and opened a photo of Leesa from the set.

Linnea nodded. "I've seen her a couple times. They even ate dinner with us."

"Can you tell me specifically when?" Jake was likely to corroborate his girlfriend's story to keep her out of prison. Linnea as a witness would be much better.

She glanced toward the ceiling as she appeared to calculate the days in her head. "Three days ago. It was after your first day of filming. I remember because Florian texted me to say they'd wrapped for the day. Jake and Leesa were at the table for hours drinking wine after we ate. The kids went to their rooms because they were put off by the PDA involved."

Leesa's alibi seemed intact. "I'd like to speak to Jake. Do you know if he's here?"

"Not sure. Try upstairs. First room on the right. I'll check my calendar while you're up there, to see if I can pinpoint the other time I saw her. I do so much running in and out of the house, I need to look at the kids' schedule to figure it out." She looked at me and smiled. "You're a single mom, too. You know what it's like."

"I'm glad I don't have to multiply it by two." I drank the remainder of my iced tea and placed the glass in the sink. "I know you didn't ask me, but I think you should use magic if it makes your life easier. Don't worry about Rick. He loves you. He'll get over it."

Linnea smiled faintly. "He does love me."

"I've got one more question before I go. Any chance you've heard of someone called Myrtle who likes to make soup out of our unsuspecting youth?"

Linnea's brow wrinkled. "Are you writing a fairy tale or something?"

"No, it's for a job."

"I haven't heard of her, but that doesn't mean much."

"No big deal, thanks."

I walked to the foyer and upstairs to the guest rooms. I knocked on the first door on the right and waited. Finally the door cracked open.

"Hey, babe. I didn't expect you..." Jake stopped when he noticed me. His light brown hair was spiked up in the front thanks to the wonders of mousse and his muscles appeared to have been poured into his snug T-shirt like concrete. "You're not Leesa."

"No, I'm Ember."

"Ember. She mentioned you."

"Yes. Like your girlfriend, I'm competing for Sheridan."

He scowled. "That guy could never get a girl like Leesa in the real world. What are you doing here? I thought Leesa and I were keeping our relationship a secret."

"I'd like to talk to you about that."

He glanced behind me as though afraid there'd be a camera crew. "I guess so. Does Leesa know you're here?"

"No, and if she did, she'd freak out and tell you to do the wrong thing."

"What's the wrong thing?"

I brushed past him into the room. "Lie. She said she was with you during the time of the murder."

He dragged a hand through his spiked hair. Unsurprisingly, the hair didn't move. "Yeah, crazy stuff, right? That Sheridan is such a tool. Who would kill over him?"

It seemed someone had been smacked in the face with the jealousy stick.

"You do realize the police suspect her because they think she has no alibi." I gauged his reaction.

"She told me to stay quiet." He narrowed his eyes at me. "Is that why you're here? You're trying to ruin her chances by ratting us out?" He whistled. "Man, I know some of those women are hardcore, but that seems really underhanded."

"It's not because I'm determined to win. It's because I'm determined to help the police find the killer. Please go to Sheriff Nash and tell him the truth. He's a good guy. The best there is, really. I'm sure if you ask him to keep the information quiet from the production team, he'll honor your request."

He eyed me closely. "If he's so awesome, then why are you in the market for a jerk like Sheridan?"

"Maybe I'm more like Leesa than you think." I let the words settle between us.

"Did you know the one who died? Were you friends or something?"

"No, but that's not the point. There's a killer among us. What if they strike again? Could you live with yourself if something happened to Leesa and you'd had the opportunity to prevent it?"

Jake flinched. "When you put it that way…"

I inclined my head toward the phone on the end table. "Call the sheriff and tell him. Let the investigation focus on actual suspects. You won't like seeing your girlfriend in an orange jumpsuit. Trust me."

"No, she hates the color orange. It makes her skin look too pink. You've convinced me." He scooped up the phone and lifted a finger to dial. "Is there a way to be patched through to the hot cop? I saw her at the beach the other day. If I have to talk to one of them, it might as well be her."

"I'm sure Leesa would be thrilled to hear your logic."

He cursed under his breath. "I really should've kept that

to myself." He banged the heel of his hand against his forehead. "Think before you speak, Jake."

"Good luck, Jake. I'll show myself out."

My work here was done.

11

I glanced at my reflection in the mirror above the console table in the dining room. I seemed to have aged exponentially this week. My hair didn't help. The frizz was in full force and I couldn't even blame the humidity since Starry Hollow didn't have any.

I've got you, boo.

I looked down to see a packet for a hydrating facial mask clenched between Raoul's paws. "Do I look that bad?"

Don't forget, the camera adds ten circles under your eyes. In my world, that's a bonus, but you're not seducing a raccoon.

"I'm not seducing anybody. I'm doing a job. That's all."

Like Julia Roberts in that movie with the man who squints a lot.

It took me a minute. "Pretty Woman?"

He perked up. *That's the one.*

I snatched the packet from him. "You just called me a hooker."

But with a heart of gold. He pursed his raccoon mouth. *Okay, maybe not so much like you.*

I tore open the packet and examined the lavender mask.

"Thanks for the help. Florian thinks I look a decade older than the other women there."

That's because you don't moisturize enough. Another year and you'll look like Artemis Haverford.

I whipped toward him with the mask firmly in place. "Say that to my face."

Raoul cowered. *I'm too pretty to die.*

Marley walked into the room and immediately dropped her book. "What's the matter with your face?"

"It's thirsty."

"If you go back to the show like that, you'll be eliminated," Marley warned.

"I have no intention of going anywhere like this. It's only for…" I glanced at Raoul who held up both paws twice. "Twenty minutes."

"You don't even like Sheridan. Why go to so much trouble?"

"I'm not used to being surrounded by a bunch of young, beautiful women."

Marley burst into laughter. "Have you forgotten what Aster and Linnea look like? When we first met them, we thought they were magical supermodels."

"I guess I've gotten used to seeing them. Their looks don't pack the same punch." They were still otherworldly gorgeous like all the members of the Rose family. Well, almost all. I took after my mother.

Marley folded her arms and looked at me with eyes far too sharp for a witch her age. "Is this about the sheriff?"

I shot her a quick glance. "What do you mean?"

"I mean you're not acting like yourself. Since when do you care how you look compared to other women?"

I pointed to my familiar. "It's his fault. He brought the mask."

Marley ignored my attempt at a redirect. "The sheriff's seeing you in the midst of all these other women. Maybe you're worried he'll start making comparisons. Unfavorable comparisons."

I opened mouth for a smart comeback but quickly snapped it closed again. Maybe Marley was right. Maybe I *was* worried.

I started to remove the mask but Raoul stopped me. *You have no idea what I had to go through to get that.*

My fingers froze an inch from the mask. "Where exactly did you get this?"

The bin outside the salon. The expensive one, though, not the cheap place. And it was still in the package.

I peeled the mask off my face. "I think the moisture has had enough time to penetrate my skin." I tried not to think about what else my skin might have absorbed.

Marley gestured to the dining table. "Whose phone is that?"

"Someone called Harold."

"The guy Marigold hired you to find?"

I nodded. "I had to charge his phone so I could look through his recent text messages." I was hoping to find a clue as to his whereabouts or, at the very least, more information on Myrtle. So far I'd come up empty-handed.

"Find anything?"

"Not yet."

"Did you check his photos?" Marley began to scroll. "He seems to have a deep love of inappropriate memes."

"Then stop scrolling. Now."

Marley placed the phone back on the table. "I don't think the phone is going to tell you anything other than Harold is incredibly immature for his age."

I rubbed the remaining moisture into my cheeks and forehead. "I have to hunt down this Myrtle."

"Who?"

"She allegedly cooks kids in her cauldron of soup. And somehow there's a turtle involved."

Marley grimaced. "Gee, thanks for the nightmare."

"Artemis gave me a lead, but I'm not sure she's the right Myrtle."

"Do you want me to ask Jinx? She knows a lot about everybody in town. She knew about our rift with Aunt Hyacinth." Marley was already typing on her phone.

It didn't surprise me that our family squabbles were fodder for town gossip. "That's okay. It's my job. I'll handle it." I paused. "Why don't you invite Jinx over for dinner one night? I'd like to meet her."

"Aren't you too busy with the show?"

"I anticipate at least one free night for dinner on the schedule."

Her expression turned hopeful. "Can we order pizza?"

"Why? Because I'm a terrible cook and you don't want me to embarrass you?"

"No, because I'd like Raoul to join us. Jinx is super excited that you have a raccoon familiar. She thinks it's rad."

"Rad, huh?" Maybe old terms were new again.

The raccoon straightened. *I like this Jinx. Who is she again?*

"What kind of pizza should I order? Please don't say Hawaiian or we'll have to rethink this friendship."

Marley arched an eyebrow. "That's the hill you're willing to die on?"

"Absolutely, as should anyone who actually enjoys pizza."

I think your terms are a bit harsh. I've had much worse on my pizza.

"What can you tell me about her parents?" I asked.

"Her mom's name is Twila and her dad is Jasper. She has a younger brother named Shale. He's in the grade below mine."

"They sound vaguely familiar."

"They should. Her parents attend the monthly coven meetings."

Unlike me. "You said they know about our rift. Are they on Team Hyacinth?"

Marley shrugged. "We don't talk about that kind of stuff in any detail."

Interesting. "What do you talk about?"

"Magic. Jinx loves it as much as I do. She's insanely talented."

"If you think that, then she must be."

Marley beamed. "She's in all the advanced classes, which is great for me because she's giving me all her notes for when I take them."

"It's handy to know someone ahead of you. What about your other friends? Do they like her?"

Marley grew quiet. "Sure."

Her response was unconvincing. "Marley, you haven't done that classic move of ditching your friends when a better one comes along, have you?"

"It isn't that I've ditched them. They just don't share the same level of interest in magic that Jinx and I do. We would bore them."

I could sort of understand that. Still, I didn't want Jinx to graduate and leave Marley without friends in a couple years.

"Try not to be too narrowly focused. Spend time doing

magic with Jinx, but then do another activity with your friends, like play music. Have you been practicing?"

Marley nodded. "A bit."

"It's best not to get consumed by one thing. It's good to be passionate, but you don't want to develop tunnel vision where you end up missing out on a bunch of other great things."

She smiled. "Whatever you say, O wise one."

"I'm not wise, just experienced in screwing up. I'd like to save you from the pain and frustration."

She regarded me. "Did you ever get consumed by something you shouldn't have?"

"Does sex with your dad count?"

She pressed her hands to her ears and screeched. "Mom, don't!"

I laughed with devilish glee. I couldn't help myself. "Your dad liked redheads," I blurted. Well, she wanted to know more stories about him.

Marley's eyebrows shot up like two airlifted caterpillars. "Come again?"

"Your dad. He had a thing for redheads. He would've gone nuts for Emma Stone."

"But you're not a redhead."

"No, but if he were alive today and in Sheridan's shoes, I bet he'd go for Ashley."

Marley's smile was so electric, she could've powered the whole cottage. "Show me."

I grabbed my phone and started scrolling through photos I'd taken. "Here she is. She likes to talk about her journey like she's Magellan."

Marley joined me to peer over my shoulder. "Oh, her. Well, Dad would have his work cut out for him. She seemed really into her boyfriend."

It took me a moment to process her statement. "What are you talking about?"

"I may also have noticed her making out with him by the rose bushes on the side of the house."

I stared at her. "The side of what house?"

She motioned in the direction of the main house. "We basically live in the backyard of Thornhold, remember?"

I narrowed my gaze. "Marley Rose, were you spying?"

Her expression turned sheepish. "I *may* have snuck over and peeked in the windows the night you filmed there." She twirled a strand of hair around her finger. "I have to be honest, I expected the guy to be better-looking. Or at least taller."

"He's reasonably tall. Maybe six-two?"

"Not the guy I saw. He was short. And he wore a green beanie which didn't do much to improve his masculinity."

"A green beanie? Sounds like the executive producer."

"Really? Is that allowed?"

I frowned. "Are you sure it was this woman?"

"Pretty sure. Show me the photos again."

I let her scroll through the camera roll. "Yes, it was definitely her."

Kristoff Mink was making out with Ashley in the rose bushes the evening of the murder. I couldn't decide whether that made one of them more or less likely to be a suspect. If their relationship was a secret and Tish found out…

I closed the camera roll. "Thanks, sweetheart. That's incredibly helpful."

"Did I just identify the killer? Because if so, I want full credit."

"Remains to be seen."

While we're on the subject of confessing to things we

shouldn't have done, there's something you should know, Raoul said.

"What else?"

When I was looking for a gift for Fancy Nancy, I may have rummaged through the garbage bins at Thornhold.

"Raoul! You know those are off limits. Aunt Hyacinth has expressly forbidden it."

I know, but I figured if Darth Vader was out of town that I could get away with it.

"Let me guess. She had the bins spelled."

Not exactly. He produced a folded sheet of paper and handed it to me. *I found this.*

I unfolded the paper and scanned the contents. "This is information about Two Rivers."

Marley glanced at the paper. "I thought Florian said she went...Well, I can't remember, but it wasn't Two Rivers."

I shrugged. "Maybe she considered it but decided to go to Two Rivers instead. This only suggests that she looked into it, not that she went." I frowned at the paper. "Although I don't know what's here that she'd want to visit. It seems like more of an artists' colony. Lots of meditation and crafts."

"That doesn't sound like Aunt Hyacinth."

"Maybe she was researching it for you or one of the grandchildren." I tossed the sheet of paper on the table. "How did Fancy Nancy like her gift?"

I'll have to let you know later. I'm giving it to her tonight if she shows up.

"Why wouldn't she show up?"

He shrugged. *We seem to have what some might refer to as a failure to communicate.*

I knew all about that. "Good luck." It occurred to me that Raoul was uniquely positioned to know whether there was a woman in town who used unusual ingredients in her cooking. "Have you heard of Myrtle, an old woman who cooks young men in soup?"

No, but now I'm hungry for soup.

My phone pinged with a message from Adrian. They wanted me to report to Haverford House in two hours for filming. Artemis had come through. As eager as I was to speak to a certain redhead whose journey took a detour through Thornhold's rosebushes, it made sense to table that conversation until later. In the meantime, I'd head for the cottage by the sea and hope I didn't end up in a cauldron of hot water.

12

The cottage by the sea looked like a dream home. The cheerful purple door and rustic 'welcome' sign didn't suggest a woman who dined on the bones of elves named Harold. There were flower boxes in the windows and a neatly cut lawn, as well as an inviting swing on the porch. Maybe it was all by design.

I strode to the front door and rang the bell. The bark of a dog took me by surprise. Canine companions weren't as common in Starry Hollow due to the variety of paranormals. Domestic dogs didn't react favorably to werewolves in particular. I'd learned this firsthand, although PP3 had mellowed since our arrival.

The door opened to reveal a short, stout woman with curly gray hair that reminded me of a statesman's wig from Colonial America. She wore a yellow dress with white daisies that ended at her ankles. Her feet were bare. Her toenails were painted sunflower yellow. Would a serial killer paint her toenails sunflower yellow? I was about to find out.

"Are you Myrtle?"

She peered at me through the screen door. "Who wants to know?"

"My name is Ember Rose. I'd like to ask you a few questions about a young man who's been missing."

Her face hardened. "What's that got to do with me?"

"Maybe nothing. Or maybe you know something that might help me find him."

"Sometimes folks are missing because they don't want to be found. Ever think of that?"

A dog appeared beside her and barked, wagging his tail at the same time. Two crystal blue eyes focused on me.

"I love Huskies," I exclaimed.

Myrtle smiled and cast an affectionate glance at the dog. "His name's Ben."

"Ben?" For a fleeting moment, I worried that Ben had once been a strapping young man who was now trapped in the form of a dog and forced to serve at Myrtle's side, but I sensed no magic at work.

Myrtle patted his head. "I adopted him from the human world. He'd been abandoned by his carers and left for dead on the side of the road."

"That's awful."

She nodded. "Found him on I-676 in Philadelphia so I named him Ben."

"After Benjamin Franklin."

Myrtle shot me a quizzical look. "That's right. You know your human history."

"I should hope so. I was raised not too far from Philadelphia."

The Siberian Husky seemed quite happy with his current situation. If he'd been spelled, he didn't seem bothered by it.

"You're lucky to have found each other."

Myrtle shifted her smile to me. "That's how I look at it, too."

"I have a dog. He's a Yorkshire terrier."

Myrtle seemed to view me in a new light. "Why don't you come in?"

She opened the door and I crossed the threshold. At least Marley and Raoul knew where I'd gone. If I failed to turn up at Haverford House later, they'd know where to start the search.

"Can I offer you a drink?"

"I'm fine, thanks."

Ben nudged my hand, encouraging me to pet him. I stroked his lush fur.

"Oh, he likes you." Myrtle bustled into the living room. "Come and sit. Tell me what you'd like to know. Maybe I can help."

It was when she turned that I noticed the odd set of her shoulders. Although there were no wings, I sensed there'd once been a rather large pair. She still walked as though carrying a heavy burden. I was dying to ask questions, but I refrained. I had other priorities.

"I'm looking for a young elf called Harold. He does yard work in town."

Her face remained impassive. "Yes, Harold. He mows my lawn."

"Has he been here recently?" The manicured state of her lawn suggested he had.

"Somewhat. Three or four days ago, I think it was."

"Did you notice anything out of the ordinary?"

"We exchanged a few words, but I don't recall anything unusual. We chatted about the weather. He gave Ben a treat." She smiled. "He always brings a treat for Ben."

I spotted a bowl of candy on the console table against

the wall. "Looks like Harold isn't the only one giving out treats."

She followed my gaze to the bowl. "I get the occasional small visitor. Children passing by on their way to explore a cove. I like to spoil them."

Spoil—or lure them? I surveyed the interior of the cottage with fresh eyes, searching for clues. If Myrtle had a history of devouring children, there was likely to be evidence. The living room was fairly nondescript. The walls were painted a creamy white and the decor was minimal. A mirror. A framed painting of a beach.

"Is that Balefire Beach?"

She followed my gaze to the painting and smiled. "It is. What do you think of it?"

"Well, I recognized it, so I'd say it's pretty good."

"I painted it last year. Balefire Beach is one of my favorite spots in Starry Hollow."

"Really? But you have that gorgeous view from here." I waved a hand in the direction of the ocean.

"Oh, I know, but this is a solitary place. I like to go to the beach and watch the families."

Watch—or stalk?

It was time to explore another room. The most likely place to find evidence was the kitchen. I stretched my arms over my head. "You know what? I wouldn't mind that drink after all."

Myrtle rose to her feet. "Why don't you join me in the kitchen? I'll make a pot of tea."

"Perfect."

I followed her into what Aunt Hyacinth would describe as a 'working kitchen.' There were no fancy kettles with mahogany handles. Cast iron pots and pans hung from the ceiling. A broom stood in the corner, presumably used to sweep the wooden floors that collected dust and crumbs.

Most significantly, there was a huge pot on the stovetop but no sign of a cauldron. I couldn't decide how to interpret it. A cauldron wasn't necessary and the pot was large enough to accommodate...Well, I didn't want to pursue that line of thought.

Myrtle filled the kettle and turned on a burner.

"Balefire Beach is one of my favorite spots, too," I said. "I take my daughter there sometimes. She loves to ride the waves on a board."

Her brow lifted. "You have a daughter? How old?"

Hmm. That was probably the wrong detail to divulge. I opted to be evasive. "She attends the Black Cloak Academy. She's a very talented witch." *So don't even think about targeting her for your next meal.*

"Was she born here?"

"No, but she definitely considers it home."

"Same. I moved here a few decades ago. Best decision I ever made." She opened the cupboard and removed two dainty teacups painted with purple and pink flowers.

"What made you decide on Starry Hollow?"

She set down the cups and waved a hand at the picture window. "I think the view speaks for itself."

Fair enough. "It sure beats New Jersey."

Myrtle gasped. "You poor girl. When you said Philadelphia, I didn't realize you meant New Jersey. And here I thought my backstory was tragic."

I latched on to her description. "Tragic?"

Myrtle seemed to realize she'd said too much. "Oh, don't mind me. I'm exaggerating."

The expression on her face suggested otherwise. Something horrible had happened to Myrtle to make her leave her hometown. Maybe she'd eaten one small child too many and the residents had forced her out.

"I didn't choose to leave New Jersey. It happened unexpectedly."

"What happened?"

"There was a bad man after me. He tried to kill Marley, that's my daughter, and me. And our little dog, too."

"Why did a man try to kill you?"

"I had to take away his prized vehicle for professional reasons and he didn't like it." Jimmy the Lighter was also a mobster—and a monster. "He set my apartment on fire. We only survived because my cousins used magic to come and rescue us."

I left out the salient details—that, at the time, we didn't know the cousins existed. That my father had hidden me from Aunt Hyacinth. It was only when I was in grave danger that my magic burst forth and broke the protective spell around me, allowing my aunt to learn my whereabouts and send for me at an opportune time.

"They whisked us away to Starry Hollow and the rest is history."

Myrtle observed me for a long moment. She seemed to be wrestling with what to say next. Finally, she drew a shaky breath and said, "How wonderful for you. I wish someone had rescued me. I had to make it out of Bluebell on my own."

"Bluebell? That's the name of your hometown?"

She pursed her wrinkled lips. "We were famous for our wild flowers. There were fields and meadows everywhere you looked, as far as the eye could see." She motioned to the teacups. "Some of them looked just like the ones painted there."

"They must've been beautiful."

Her face clouded over. "Even beautiful things can be tainted by darkness."

"What happened to you, Myrtle? Whatever it is, I'm guessing it wasn't sunshine and unicorns."

She removed the screeching kettle from the burner and poured the boiling water into two cups. "Definitely not. There was a plant that grew there called fairy fernseed. Have you heard of it?"

I shook my head. I took the opportunity to ask the question that had been burning my tongue. "You're a fairy?"

She hesitated. "Yes. Sometimes I wonder whether I ought to say I'm something else. Can you still be a fairy without fairy wings?"

"I'd still be a witch even without a wand."

She cast a sidelong glance at me. "But would you still be a witch without magic?"

I wasn't sure it was comparable, but I let Myrtle continue talking.

"Occasionally people came to Bluebell from the human world to find the fernseed. I don't know how they knew about the plant or how to cross into Bluebell. I suspect there were local fairies that profited from the trade and encouraged the visits."

"What's special about fairy fernseed?"

"It offers the power of invisibility. No need for a spell. You simply tuck a few seeds in your pocket and you've done it." She swallowed. "I was in a meadow playing with some local children when a group of men turned up and demanded I show them where they could find fairy fernseed. I didn't like the way they eyed the children. I got the terrible feeling they'd use their powers of invisibility for nefarious purposes, so I refused."

A chill traveled down my spine. "And I guess they didn't like your response."

Her voice dropped to a hoarse whisper. "No. Not in the slightest. They attacked me. I instructed the children to run, but they were too frightened, so I used all the magic at my disposal to propel them. But it took a toll and I didn't have enough magic left to defend myself."

I winced. "They removed your wings?"

She handed me a teacup. "They tore them from my body with brute strength. I'd never felt such pain." As though sensing her distress, Ben trotted into the kitchen and panted at her. She bent down to stroke his back. It seemed that the Husky also played the role of emotional support animal.

"I'm so sorry, Myrtle. That is tragic."

She took a sip of tea from her cup. "They left me for dead. Another fairy found me bleeding to death in the meadow. Later, they scolded me for my stubbornness."

"They scolded you?"

Tears streamed down her cheeks as she nodded. "They didn't see why it mattered what the men did with the seeds. They paid one of the fairies, you see, and she felt it was no concern of ours what happened in the human world once the seeds were out of our hands. Out of sight, out of mind."

Myrtle wasn't luring children to her cottage in the hopes of eating them. She simply enjoyed their companionship.

She missed them.

"I am so sorry you went through all that. You were incredibly brave to stand up to them."

I knew with certainty that Harold wasn't here. In fact, if I told Myrtle I thought he was in trouble, I was willing to bet she'd drop everything to help me. But I wasn't about to do that. Myrtle had suffered enough. I could handle this job on my own.

"Sometimes I wonder if I'd made a different choice, what would've happened? Maybe nothing." She shrugged. "Who knows for sure? But I couldn't have lived with myself."

She'd sacrificed a part of herself to save those children. Myrtle wasn't a mysterious soup maven. She was a hero.

I glanced at the clock on my phone. I was due at Haverford House in thirty minutes. If I wanted to at least run a brush through my hair, I'd have to leave now.

I swallowed another mouthful of tea and set down the cup. "I hate to go so soon, but I have a previous engagement."

"Oh, no worries. It was so lovely to meet you. I hope you'll consider coming back for a visit when you have more time."

"Absolutely. If you don't mind, I'd like to bring my daughter, too. She would flip over your dog. She adores animals."

Myrtle lit up like the night sky on Fourth of July. "Please do. I would love that."

"If you hear anything about Harold, will you let me know?" I gave her my number.

Her hand trembled as she set down her teacup. "Now you have me worrying about him."

I curled my fingers over her hand. "I've got this, Myrtle. I may not have many talents, but if there's one thing I've learned in Starry Hollow, I can solve a puzzle."

She looked at me with a hint of uncertainty. "It's good to know your strengths. What you fail to recognize, you fail to use."

I gave her hand a gentle squeeze and gave Ben one more pat. "I'll see you again soon, Myrtle."

I left the cottage with mixed feelings. Although I was disappointed not to have generated a new lead in connection with Harold's disappearance, I was grateful to have met Myrtle and heard her story. There was no reason for her to continue to live such a solitary existence. It seemed to me we could all learn a thing or two from Myrtle's integrity and selflessness.

13

I hurried to Haverford House and prayed I wasn't late. I didn't want to jeopardize my current good standing with Sheridan. The property was already overflowing with vehicles. Artemis stood outside the house when I arrived.

"Not staying to watch?"

The elderly witch shook her head. "Too many of them swarming about like flies. It's too much for me."

"Where are you going?"

"For a walk in the woods. Jefferson will keep an eye on things in my absence."

"I just came from Myrtle's cottage."

Her brow lifted. "The one who adds children to her soup?"

"Not that one. This Myrtle loves kids in the normal sense. I think you two might hit it off. Would it be okay if I invite her over to have tea with us once this production is finished?"

Artemis nodded. "Any friend of yours is a friend of mine. You know that, Ember, dear."

I made a mental note to arrange the get-together. Myrtle

and Artemis seemed like they'd get along. It would be nice for Artemis to have a card player still in the land of the living.

"You should go inside," she urged. "It seemed like they were about to start."

As I entered the foyer, Adrian was admiring the expansive interior. "We can really film here?"

"Yes, but do we want to?" Sheridan rubbed his arms. "Is this place haunted? I'm not getting good vibes."

"Jefferson is a ghost, but he works here," I explained. "And you don't have to worry about him spying on anyone inappropriately. He only has eyes for the lady of the house."

Sheridan grimaced. "Um, I met the lady of the house. Does she have a great-granddaughter or something?"

"No, Artemis is the lady of the house. She and Jefferson have a history."

Sheridan's brow furrowed. "You know them?"

"I've spent a lot of time here." As if on cue, the cat of the house appeared and rubbed against my leg. "This is the other lady of the house, Clementine."

Sheridan crouched down to pet the cat behind the ear. She hissed and nipped at his hand before running away.

"I'm so sorry."

Sheridan sucked on the wound. "Keep this cat out of the way during filming. I don't want anybody to end up with an infection. I can't drink on antibiotics and some of these women...Let's just say I need alcohol to get through my time with them." He nudged me with his shoulder. "You're not one of them, in case you were worried."

"I wasn't worried."

Sheridan didn't react. Even so, I shook off my attitude. I couldn't afford to get eliminated tonight. I wouldn't get paid by Mrs. Sinclair, nor would I be on the inside to solve the murder. Unfortunately I had to play nice. Not one of my strengths.

I squared my shoulders and flashed a smile at Sheridan. "I'm kidding. I'm so relieved."

He returned the smile. How could he not tell I was faking my interest? I was the worst actress in the world. Maybe my skills were improving and I didn't realize it.

"Sheridan, we need you," Delilah called from the staircase.

"See you in a few minutes," he said to me.

I took the opportunity to go in search of Ashley. I found her in the kitchen and grabbed her by the elbow. "I need to talk to you."

The yoga instructor seemed taken aback. "Me?"

I steered her through the kitchen door to the outside patio and closed the door behind us. "Let's talk about your journey for a quick second."

She clasped her hands in a prayer position. "Oh, I'm so thrilled you're interested. I got the distinct impression that you found me boring."

"Oh, I do, but then I found out you were swapping spit with Kristoff and you suddenly became more interesting."

Her mask of innocence fell away. "Who told you about us?"

"Doesn't matter. So what happened? You killed her together as some sort of sick game? She found out about the two of you and threatened to report it? You killed off the competition and asked him to cover for you?"

Ashley sucked in a horrified breath. "You can't be serious. Do you really think I'd risk everything to bump off one woman? I'd have to detonate a bomb and get rid of all my competition in one fell swoop."

I raised my eyebrows. "Sounds like you've given that some thought."

She placed a hand on her hip. "You can't prove there's anything going on between Kristoff and me."

"That's quite the sharp left turn on your spiritual path, Ashley."

"I didn't intend for it to happen. Kris and I connected on another level."

"Only because his head comes up to your chest."

She ignored my remark. "You can't tell anybody, please. It's a huge secret for obvious reasons."

"Doesn't it bother him that you're in a competition to marry another man?"

"He doesn't want to derail my dream. He's letting me compete and then we'll pick up where we left off after the show ends."

"Letting you?"

"As the executive producer, not as my boyfriend."

"And what if you win?"

"All journeys have bridges to cross."

I kept my eyes from rolling. "Where were you when Tish was killed?"

"With Kris."

"In the bushes?" At least they would have smelled like roses afterward. Those thorns, though.

"No. That was earlier. We were in the master bedroom together."

I choked back laughter. "You were upstairs in the master suite?" Did Ashley and Kristoff have sex in Aunt Hyacinth's bed? The mere prospect sent me into a fit of giggles. Very mature, I know.

"Yes, we were so consumed with each other, we didn't hear anything until the deputy arrived and started sealing off the area. We snuck out the upstairs window and climbed down the vines."

"What did you tell the sheriff?"

"That I was en route to meet the other girls at a club."

"And what did Kristoff say?"

"That he was in a meeting with Adrian at a pub."

Which meant Adrian had also lied. So was Adrian actually alone—or with Tish during her final moments?

"Talk to Kristoff. I'm sure he'll bargain for your silence, although he won't promise to let you win. It's the one thing he won't compromise." She paused. "Not even for me."

"You asked?"

"Of course. In fact, it's the reason I slept with him in the first place. I didn't expect to fall for him."

Adrian's head poked outside. "It's time, ladies."

Speak of the devil. I'd have to get a word in with him later.

We returned to the house to find cameras and lights set up in the parlor room. Sheridan stood in front of the windows and the contestants were lined up across the room opposite him.

"This house is so well-preserved," Daisy said. "I'd love to live in a place like this someday."

"Your current house isn't an antique?" Leesa asked.

Daisy cringed. "I live in a studio apartment with a kitchenette. I don't even have a full kitchen. I am the queen of microwaveable meals and smoothies in the blender."

"That part must keep you healthy. Upside," I said.

"I think this place is creepy," Alyx interjected. "It feels like the walls are watching us, judging us."

I didn't doubt Jefferson was judging her. She was a real piece of work.

"We're ready to roll. Let's get started," Adrian announced.

"I'd better win the date night this time," Alyx said, shooting me a haughty look. "The topic is fitness, which puts me way ahead of the rest of you."

"You've got me there," I said. "I only run when chased."

"And how often does that happen?" Alyx scoffed.

"More often than you would think," I replied, remembering all the times I'd ended up in a showdown with a criminal. Even before moving to Starry Hollow, I'd done more than my fair share of running from people. As a repo agent, I claimed cars that owners were determined to keep.

The cameras started to roll. Kristoff greeted us and instructed Delilah to hand out sneakers in our respective sizes because today's competition involved an obstacle course that the crew had set up in the backyard.

I didn't even try to win this one. There was a climbing wall, a mud pit, and a rope that required upper body strength. By the time I finished last, I needed two showers and a bottle of bleach. To Alyx's shock and dismay, Ashley ended up winning the competition and, thus, the next date with Sheridan.

Murmurs drew my attention across the yard. It only took a moment to understand the reason. Bianca strode toward us. She wore a red dress with a plunging neckline that would've put Scarlett O'Hara to shame. Her glamorous appearance was in stark contrast to the rest of us who looked like we'd been dragged through the mud—because we had.

"What's Bianca doing here?" Ashley asked. "She was eliminated."

"Stop filming," Daisy demanded. "She doesn't belong here."

No one responded.

Leesa moved to block her path. "Bianca, I know you have the memory of a goldfish, but I'm here to remind you that you didn't get chosen."

Bianca simply smiled and skirted the curvaceous obstacle.

Sheridan offered a nervous grin. "Hey, B. What are you doing back?"

"Coming for a second chance." She flashed a fanged smile at the camera. "Doesn't everybody deserve one?"

Ugh, the baby voice was back.

"Normally I would agree with you, but that's not within the spirit of the competition," Ashley said.

"I'd like the opportunity to prove myself. Have a date with me and then decide."

Sheridan made a noise at the back of his throat. "My date tonight is with Ashley."

I felt compelled to speak up on behalf of my client, if no one else. "Bianca, you're embarrassing yourself. Sheridan didn't choose you. In fact, he specifically chose not to keep you in the mix. Do us all a favor and go before things get uncomfortable."

Bianca folded her arms. "I am *not* leaving. If you want me out of here, you'll have to do it by force."

Deputy Valentina Pitt stepped forward. I had no idea when the security detail had arrived. "I'll take that action," she said.

Sheridan grinned at the sight of the sexy deputy. "Same."

The deputy whipped out a set of handcuffs. "We can do this the easy way or the hard way."

Sheridan's eyes widened. "Please say the hard way."

Daisy smacked his arm. I didn't blame her. If I'd been closer to him, I would've done the same.

Bianca's jaw tightened. "I deserve another chance. I was eliminated too soon."

"That's how the game works," Leesa said. "Somebody has to go each round and this time it was you."

Bianca glared at her. "Someone sabotaged my cosmetics. If I'd had the makeup I'd intended, I wouldn't have been the one to go."

"Bianca, I didn't eliminate you because your eyeshadow was too dark or whatever," Sheridan interrupted.

She sauntered closer to him, hips swaying provocatively. "Then why did you? It couldn't be based on appearances because I'm a ten in a yard full of sixes." She cast a glance over her shoulder at the other women. "And that's being generous."

Daisy shot a helpless look at the producers. "Kristoff?"

The leprechaun ventured forward. "We've talked it over and we're going to leave the decision up to Sheridan."

Sheridan puffed out his chest. "I'll give Bianca another chance."

A collective gasp followed his announcement.

"But it's my date night with you," Ashley whined.

"Not anymore." Bianca flashed a devilish smile and looped her arm through Sheridan's. "Where are you taking me?"

Sheridan couldn't seem to look at her face. He was too busy staring at her ample cleavage. "Anywhere you want, B."

Ashley turned to the producer and held out her hands in despair. The producer silently shook his head. The wereass was letting this play out. I actually felt bad for Ashley.

"He isn't worth this," Jackie exploded. "He's like a duke when we should be gunning for a prince." She whipped toward Sheridan. "Look at the mud on my arms. It's disgusting." She held out her arms for examination. I spotted a few flecks of dirt. Nothing like my own mud-caked extremities.

"If I'm not worth it, then maybe you should take Bianca's place," Sheridan said in a steely voice.

Jackie seemed to come to her senses. "I'm sorry. I don't know what came over me. It's the stress." She promptly burst into tears and ran toward the house.

"Why don't you take both women on the date?" Leesa suggested. "Make it a double."

Sheridan nodded his approval. "Great idea." He snaked a hand around Bianca's waist and made eye contact with Ashley. "You don't mind, do you?"

Ashley looked ready to barf. "No, of course not. My shaman says I have a generous spirit."

Sheridan wiggled his fingers at her and she reluctantly joined the couple.

"Have a great date," Leesa said, clearly relishing the outcome.

Daisy's mouth hung open. She clearly seemed stunned by the decision. Why she expected better of Sheridan, I had no idea.

Leesa seemed to notice Daisy's crestfallen expression.

"This is a great development for us," Leesa assured her. "Neither one of them will get enough of his attention and he'll end up eliminating both of them. He already ditched Bianca once and if I never have to hear that baby voice again, I'll be thrilled."

I watched Bianca carefully as she stroked Sheridan's arm. If she was stubborn enough to come back to the set after she was booted, was she stubborn enough to kill off the competition? I'd ruled out Ashley, but Bianca didn't know the truth about the yoga instructor's journey. If Bianca was the killer, Ashley might be in danger tonight.

"Here's the kicker," Kristoff said. "At the end of the date, Sheridan will have to choose one of you to go home."

The tension in the air was palpable.

"Any of us?" Daisy asked.

"No, he'll have to choose between Bianca and Ashley."

Daisy relaxed. Ashley, on the other hand, turned a little bit greener, and Bianca's smile widened.

Kristoff explained their double date would involve spelunking and exploring local caves.

"But it'll be dark soon," Ashley interjected.

I had a feeling there'd be a candlelit table for two waiting for them in one of the caves unless Adrian managed to sneak in there and add a third chair in time. Awkward.

"I love the dark," Bianca said, casting a sultry look at Sheridan. "In fact, I'm at my best in the dark."

Good grief.

As Adrian gave the trio directions to the date site, I inched closer to eavesdrop. It seemed dangerous to let Ashley climb slippery rocks in the dark in the company of a potential killer, which meant I was left with one choice—stalker mode, activated.

THE PRODUCERS CHOSE a series of caves near Mermaid Cove that made for excellent spelunking. Each participant wore a hard hat fitted with a GoPro-type device to capture every minute of the date, later to be whittled down to the few exciting or dramatic ones during the editing process. If Bianca was planning to do anything sneaky, it would be easy enough for her to dispose of the devices.

With my broomstick at my feet, I observed the trio from

behind a boulder in the cove. They were already scaling one of the cliffs to reach a cave. Bianca kept inching closer to Sheridan. Ashley was athletic enough to win the obstacle course race, but Bianca was a vampire. If she'd participated in the obstacle course, she would've won without great effort. Watching her now, the vampire's movements were strong and fluid. As long as Sheridan stayed between them, Ashley would be safe from harm—at least from Bianca. The slick rocks were another story.

Bianca must have decided to impress Sheridan with her prowess because she climbed straight past the first cave and continued to the higher one. She was trying to lose Ashley. She figured the yoga instructor would decide to call it quits at the first cave and Bianca would have the rest of the date to herself. Cunning.

I waited until Ashley and Sheridan entered the first cave to make my move. Bianca was alone, but not for very long. I had to seize the moment or lose it. I mounted my broom and flew straight through the mouth of the upper cave. I landed with a bump and knocked my tailbone against the wooden stick. Not my finest moment.

Startled by my sudden appearance, the vampire jumped. "You? What on earth are you doing? There's already two of us on this stupid date."

"Relax. I think you've managed to edge out Ashley."

Bianca smiled, appearing pleased. "What makes you say that?"

"Ashley is nice enough, but she doesn't have enough of a personality for him."

Bianca thrust out her chest. "I have more than enough for both of us."

"So I see."

She regarded me with suspicion. "What are you doing

here then? You didn't come all the way up here to give me an update."

"No." I joined her at the small table. "I was hoping to talk to you in private before the cameras catch up to you." I glanced at the camera on her hat.

"Don't worry. It's off. I switched it off when I got here so that I could practice my speech."

"Your speech?"

Her mouth quirked. "You know—the big romantic gesture the audience will love."

"Got it." I didn't have the heart to tell her the audience wasn't going to love anything she did. I could see Bianca becoming the villain of the production without much need for editing. "I have a couple questions."

"Is this about my return? Because it wasn't my idea. Kristoff put me up to it."

I smacked my head. Of course he did. It made perfect sense. The leprechaun didn't want Ashley to have a solo date with Sheridan so he was perfectly content to let Bianca disrupt the event.

"It isn't about that." Although knowing Bianca didn't decide to return on her own made me less inclined to see her as the killer. "It's about Tish."

"The dead woman? Why would you climb into a cave to ask me about her?"

"Doesn't it concern you that no one's been arrested for her murder?"

Her eyes glinted in the dimly lit cave. "Why does that sound like code for an accusation?"

"It's not an accusation. I'm asking, that's all."

She removed the hat from her head and placed it on the small table. "I'm a vampire. If I were going to kill someone, I'd use the gifts the gods gave me." She flicked a sharp fang.

"Puncture wounds would've been obvious. If you wanted to escape detection, you would've made sure to kill her some other way to deflect blame."

She grimaced. "But poison?"

"The weapon of choice for a lady they used to call it." Or something like that.

Bianca crossed her legs. "I'm no lady, and I had nothing to do with what happened to Tish. I want to win, but not that badly. I'm a ten. If I want a hot, rich guy, I can get one." She tossed her hair over her shoulder. "One far better than Sheridan Sinclair."

"Then why pursue one on national television?"

She flashed a coy smile. "Why not? Better tables at restaurants. More followers on social media. All of it increases my attractiveness to other men, even if I lose."

I decided to ask the other question that had been nagging at me. "Why the baby voice?"

She shrugged. "Men like to take care of weak women. Makes them feel stronger. More powerful. The voice helps."

I wasn't sure I agreed, but her answer was interesting nonetheless.

"You sounded very accomplished. A good education in the human world, job offers. Why do you need a man to take care of you?"

"I don't need one. I want one. And I don't know the first thing about poison, but I'll tell you this. If I were to poison my rival, I'd use her lipstick. Let her rub it all over her lips and die by her own hand."

I stared at her. The sheriff's team still hadn't figured out how the poison had been administered. What if Bianca was on to something? I pulled out my phone.

Bianca frowned. "Who are you calling?"

"I'm sending a quick text to a friend." I hurriedly passed

the idea to Sheriff Nash to investigate. "Just out of curiosity, where were you at the time of the murder?"

"The police already asked me and I told them the truth. I went straight from Thornhold to the blood bank. I wanted an extra supply in case I scored an overnight with Sheridan. I get hangry when I haven't had enough blood and I didn't want to embarrass myself."

"Were you able to prove it?"

She offered a flirtatious smile. "I'm sure the staff remembered me. I was better dressed than their usual customer."

"Did you happen to catch the names of the paranormals working?"

"One was called John. I know because he gave me his phone number. I didn't have the heart to tell him I don't date anybody who works in retail."

I wasn't sure the blood bank counted as retail, but it didn't seem worth arguing the point.

"Not to be cruel about the dead woman, but I don't understand why anyone would single out Tish as a frontrunner to eliminate. If they were going to target anyone, it should've been me."

The virtue of modesty seemed to have escaped her.

Her gaze flicked over me. "He seems to have taken a liking to you, though. I guess he's drawn to powerful women."

"What makes you think I'm powerful?"

Her nostrils flared. "Are you serious? You reek of it. Any vampire with half a nose can smell it on you. Maybe nymphs can sense it, too."

I cocked my head and examined her. "Who do you think killed Tish?"

She scrutinized her black-painted nails. "No idea, but it doesn't worry me one bit. If I feared for my life, I wouldn't have come back at Kristoff's request. I would've holed up in a B&B and pampered myself until the sheriff said we could leave town."

I had a hard time envisioning Bianca staying sequestered in a room. No doubt she'd be on the prowl trying to find another mark.

"Now I have a question for you. Why do you care so much about a woman you didn't know?" Bianca asked.

I met her inquisitive gaze. "She died, Bianca. She was killed right under our noses. I know death might be a tricky concept to grasp for a vampire, but her death mattered. We should care that she died and we should care who killed her."

"We'll have to agree to disagree." Bianca placed her hard hat back on her head. "I'm going to switch on the camera. If you don't want to be seen, you should probably go now."

I took the hint and vacated the cave before Ashley and Sheridan arrived. Before I even made it home, Adrian sent a group text to let us know Sheridan had elected to send Ashley packing. It seemed her Natural Selection journey was to end at Mermaid Cove. Bianca, however, lived to date another day.

14

As I flew over Thornhold, I noticed movement along the side of the house and lowered my broom to investigate. It was only when I landed that I realized I'd stumbled upon Raoul's attempt at an intimate dinner for two. Candles flickered on two overturned lids with a moth-eaten blanket between them. Raoul sat at one end of the blanket and a white cat with the finest hair you'd ever seen sat at the other. A pink collar with rhinestones was secured around her neck. She licked her paw like she was grooming herself for a television appearance. I felt a strange energy emanating from the picnic.

"Are you using magic?" I asked.

Raoul glowered at me. *You're not supposed to be here.*

Sorry. I tucked my broom under my arm and tried to creep past them in the shadows, but the cat noticed me and meowed.

"I'm not sticking around," I promised. "Just passing by on my way home." I picked up the pace. If I ruined Raoul's romantic evening, the raccoon would never forgive me.

The cat ran after me, crying loudly. I stopped and turned around. "What's wrong with her?"

Raoul's body slumped. *I don't know. I tried to make it the perfect evening, but she ate the food and then cried.*

"Maybe she's still hungry."

Let me see if I can find more tuna. He scrambled back to the picnic.

I bent over to address the cat. "Listen, Fancy Nancy, or whatever your name is. Raoul is a good guy and you'd be crazy to mistreat him. Understood?"

The cat opened her mouth and screeched. I bolted upright and backed away. "Good luck with that one," I called, and raced for home.

An unfamiliar car sat in my driveway with the motor running. The back door opened as I approached, revealing Evelyn Sinclair. Her cane rested against her leg. "I'm here for an update, my dear."

"I figured that from the ten voicemails you left me earlier."

"If you received them all, why not answer one of them?"

"Because there isn't much to report. I'm doing my best."

"You came in dead last at the obstacle course. Is that what you consider your best?"

Gods above, it was like talking to Aunt Hyacinth. "I was unlikely to win the second date anyway. And Ashley's been eliminated."

"Which one is Ashley?"

"Yogi on a journey."

"Right, Sheridan said talking to her was like interacting with a blank wall." She shifted in the seat. "I hear you're out of another location."

"What do you mean?"

"The crew was too spooked by the ghost at Haverford House. They refuse to go back."

That was too bad. "Jefferson wouldn't hurt anyone. He lives to serve." Sort of.

"Be that as it may, his presence made them too uncomfortable. They threatened to quit unless Kristoff changed locations."

I placed a hand on my hip. "And why is it that you know this information before I do?"

A knowing smile caressed her lips. "Sheridan calls me every day like the good grandson he is."

I fought the urge to roll my eyes. Not a mama's boy but a grandma's boy. I couldn't decide which one was worse.

"What else has he told you?"

"That he's tired. I told him to buck up. He got himself into this fiasco. He can ride it out."

Spoken like a true matriarch.

"I don't want to hear that you lost again. Use magic if you have to. Whatever it takes to win."

It was one thing to control the body bubbles on our date, but using magic to influence the outcome was a different story. "I can't do magic to win. It's prohibited. If it's discovered, I'll be removed from the competition and then you'll be left with…whoever's left."

She scowled. "I thought you were a clever woman. Surely you can find a way to use magic that goes undetected."

"Sheridan seems to like me well enough without any magical influence. I'd prefer to keep it that way."

She banged her cane on the car floor. "It doesn't matter whether he truly likes you. If magic will seal the deal, then I command you to use it."

Laughter escaped me. "You command me? Like a queen?"

Her eyes turned to slits. "You find that amusing?"

"That you rule over me? Yes, I do, Mrs. Sinclair. I only have two, arguably three rulers, and they're all under five-foot-two."

The older woman didn't like my response. She straightened her shoulders and looked at me with venom in her eyes. "I hired you for a job, my dear, which means you answer to me until such job has been completed."

I knocked on the driver's window. "Your boss is ready to go home now." I closed Mrs. Sinclair's door and walked away.

She rolled down the window. "I haven't finished yet."

"You can finish tomorrow." I unlocked the front door of the cottage. "I need to get to bed." Without a backward glance, I slipped inside and shut the door behind me.

Marley was already sound asleep. By the time I showered and got dressed for bed, a raccoon-shaped silhouette appeared in my bedroom doorway.

"Hey. What happened with Fancy Nancy?"

He averted his gaze. *We're over. She's been using me.*

"For what?"

Food. She doesn't seem to know how to find it without help.

"Well, she *is* wearing a fancy pink collar. Maybe she's normally fed in a jewel-encrusted bowl inside a large house. Have you asked her why she's roaming the streets?"

We seem to have a hard time communicating. I only partly understand her. It's the whole raccoon-cat thing.

"You understand Bonkers."

That's because she's Marley's familiar.

I frowned. "I don't think that's true. There've been other woodland creatures and animals at the dump…"

Raoul thrust out his paws in an agitated state. *It's me, okay? She just doesn't want to communicate with me. I'm beneath her.*

I sighed. "I'm sorry, buddy. It happens to the best of us. It might happen to me in a matter of days, in fact, although our client insists that I use any means necessary to win."

In other words, magic.

I nodded.

I can help with that.

I shifted PP3 off the pillow. "Why? More importantly, how?"

If I'm responsible for the enchantment, then technically you're not breaking any rules.

"What kind of enchantment do you have in mind?"

Let's consult the book.

I cut a glance at the clock. It was later than I preferred, but I could handle another half hour.

I followed him downstairs.

He ambled over to the altar and opened the grimoire, using his paws to page through until he found a suitable entry. *This ought to do the trick.*

"I'm not sure I want to know."

The raccoon grunted. *Get your mind out of the dumpster. I don't mean trick as in turning tricks.*

I peered over his head at the book. "A Love Poppet?"

I think they misspelled puppet.

"No, poppet is a word."

Huh. How about that? Learn something new every few weeks. He scanned the page. *We need a photo of you and him.*

"Wait. Before we start, what will it do? I don't want Sheridan to become a love zombie or anything like that." I reviewed the instructions. "This spell is designed for an existing couple. I need something that draws Sheridan to me."

Raoul flipped to the next page. *Here we go.*

I read the title—Pocket Love Charm.

The raccoon made a wolfish noise. *You're bringing sexy back with this one.*

"I don't need to bring sexy anywhere. I just need to satisfy the client and help Granger find a killer."

Might as well flaunt your sex appeal while you do it. He waved me away. *You need to go so you can have plausible deniability.*

"That's a big term for a small familiar."

I learned it from Marley.

"Dare I ask the context?"

You daren't, but it involved an empty pizza box that may or may not have belonged to me.

"Got it." I turned to walk away.

Before you go, could you grab me a red candle, High John root from the supplies, and a spool of red thread?

"What makes you think I have a spool of red thread?"

You don't, but Marley does. It's from that Valentine's Day project she worked on at school.

"When was that?"

Valentine's Day. Duh. Check the top shelf of her bedroom closet.

"How do you know what's on the top shelf of her bedroom closet?"

Because I was searching for bonus gifts and saw the sewing kit.

"What are bonus gifts?"

Gifts that I give to myself when I find them, like a toy Roman helmet with the fancy plume or the Harry Potter Monopoly board game with only half the pieces missing. Bonuses. Hence bonus gifts.

I shook my head. "You're lucky you're my familiar."

I think you mean you're lucky.

I gathered the requested items and left them at the base of the altar. "I'll leave you to it. I don't want to know any more than necessary."

Probably for the best. He craned his neck to look at me. *Is there a fire extinguisher handy, by any chance?*

My eyes widened. "Why would you ask that?"

Because the spell involves lighting a candle and you may have noticed my skills are lacking in the opposable thumb area. He held up his paws.

"If you can't light a candle without help, I don't think you'd be able to operate the extinguisher either."

In that case, you should probably hang out in the kitchen with the extinguisher ready until I give the all-clear. You might as well make us a snack while you're in there. Enchantments can build up an appetite.

I rolled my eyes. "I'll get right on it, sir."

I disappeared into the kitchen and pulled microwaveable popcorn from the pantry. To his credit, Raoul was easy to please in the food arena.

Ten minutes later the raccoon appeared in the doorway. *Here it is. Your ticket to charisma.*

I scowled. "Are you suggesting I lack charisma without a magical boost?"

Let me rephrase. Here's your ticket to Lover Town. This root will draw your lover to you. He hobbled over and placed the root on the counter. It was wrapped in red thread and small enough to fit in my pocket.

"I guess that's why they call it a pocket love charm."

He sniffed the air. *I smell salt and lots of it.* He abandoned the charm and went straight for the popcorn. Fancy Nancy didn't know what she was missing.

15

I spent the next morning going through my notes on the murder investigation, as well as the apps on Harold's phone. I was frustrated by my lack of progress. It didn't help that I still felt the sting of Mrs. Sinclair's sharp rebuke from last night. It was as though Aunt Hyacinth arranged for a replacement model while she was out of town.

After lunch, I drove to the Caffeinated Cauldron with the love charm safely in my pocket. If Adrian called me to the set at a moment's notice, I'd be ready. There were no available spots out front, so I parked on the street a couple blocks away and walked. I passed a dwarf and an elf, both of whom offered an admiring whistle as they passed. Had I forgotten to put on a bra or something? I paused to glance at my reflection in a store window. No, I looked the same as always.

"You are a vision," a deep voice said.

I turned to see a minotaur behind me. "Uh, thanks."

I continued toward the coffee shop. By the time I reached the entrance, I had a stream of paranormals trailing

Magic & Marriage 169

behind me. The door opened from the inside and Deputy Bolan appeared on the pavement.

The leprechaun immediately noticed the line behind me. "Why are they following you? Do you have mutton in your pockets or something?"

I patted my pockets as though there might actually be mutton. Instead I felt only the root that Raoul made.

Of course. The love charm. At least I knew it worked—a little too well.

"If they're harassing you, call the sheriff. I've got an appointment with my husband that I can't miss or I'll be sleeping on the sofa the rest of the week."

"They're not bothering me, but I appreciate the concern." I was from New Jersey, I'd been cat-called more in my life than Garfield. It would take a lot more than admiring glances and declarations of love to unnerve me.

"Suit yourself." The leprechaun scuttled to his patrol car.

I entered the coffee shop and the followers crammed in behind me. The temperature inside seemed to increase and beads of sweat bubbled across my brow. I spotted Alyx in the crowd of admirers. What was she doing here? I elbowed my way toward her.

"Did you get swept up in the crowd on the way? Shouldn't you be primping for Sheridan?"

Alyx gazed at me with adoration in her eyes. "Why would I want to be on a date with Sheridan when I can be here with you?"

Uh oh.

"You don't want to give up your chance with Sheridan."

She fluttered her eyelashes at me like a cartoon cat. "You'd be worth it."

Oh, boy. "Alyx, listen. You don't know what you're saying. You don't even like me, let alone want to date me."

"I like you. I noticed those amazing eyes of yours the moment you walked into Thornhold." She caressed my arm. "And I happen to have a thing for older women."

"A thing the way I have a crush on Gal Gadot or an actual thing?"

She entwined her fingers with mine. "I'm not into dudes. I told you when I met you I was only there to be on television."

What was it with these women who entered the competition for other reasons? I started to laugh, realizing what a hypocrite I was.

"What's so funny?" Alyx asked.

It occurred to me that my laughter could be misunderstood. "I'm sorry, Alyx. I'm not laughing at you. I'm just feeling sorry for Sheridan."

"It's Tish I feel sorry for. Imagine dying over that loaf of white bread."

"Maybe she didn't die over him." Although I'd yet to come up with a better reason. "I don't suppose she knew your secret."

Alyx barked a harsh laugh. "Not a chance. My secret is so safe that sometimes *I* forget I'm a lesbian."

"No girlfriend back at home then?"

"Not at the moment. I'm trying to convince my parents I'm straight so they won't write me out of their will. They're dead set on me not embarrassing the family with my sexual preferences." She used air quotes around sexual preferences. "My parents are loaded, by the way. Once I inherit the money, I plan to donate half of it to organizations that support LGBTQ-plus rights and find myself a gorgeous wife. I hope you'll consider the invitation."

Talking to Alyx while she was under a spell was like

Magic & Marriage

talking to a drunk person. She seemed willing to confess all her innermost thoughts.

"I'm flattered, really, but I'm sort of..." I halted abruptly at the sight of the sheriff coming toward me. Talk about timing.

He gave me a curious look. "What's happening, Rose? There seems to be quite the commotion and from what I can tell, you're at the center of it."

Alyx gave him a stern look. "Can't you see we're in the middle of something important?"

"And I'm in the middle of a murder investigation," the sheriff said. "Aren't you one of the suspects...I mean, contestants?"

Alyx wisely dissolved into the crowd.

"New admirers?" he asked with mild amusement.

"Kind of. There's been a little misunderstanding."

His gaze flicked to the crowd and back to me. "I'm real curious as to what that misunderstanding might be. Did you promise them all a million bucks or something?"

"I love you, Ember," a minotaur called.

"Ember, wait for me. I'll treasure you like the diamond in the rough you truly are," another one yelled.

The sheriff's eyebrows crept toward his hairline. "I'm almost afraid to ask."

"I've been practicing my...seduction skills for the show. I guess they worked better than I expected." I laughed half-heartedly.

His face turned to stone somewhere around the word 'seduction.' Gently, he took me by the elbow and steered me to the far side of the room. The crowd shouted in protest.

"Don't take the love of my life!"

"I feel so cold now!"

The sheriff frowned at them before lowering his voice. "What's really going on, Rose?"

"Is it so hard to believe all those paranormals are attracted to me?"

A smile flickered across his lips. "Not even remotely, but I don't think that's what's happening here, do you?"

I heaved a sigh. "I'll tell you, but you have to promise to keep it to yourself." I rubbed the back of my neck. "Raoul made an enchantment to help me win over Sheridan and it's stronger than we intended."

Granger cast a glance over his shoulder at the persistent group. "You don't say."

"If you're not here to order, you need to leave," the barista shouted. "We're at capacity. I don't want to have the fire marshal show up."

"While I have your attention," I began, "were you able to confirm Bianca's alibi?"

His face grew pinched. "That was the vampire at the blood bank?"

"Yes."

He nodded. "A young fellow by the name of John confirmed her story."

"And the lipstick theory?"

"No trace of poison in the victim's lipstick or cosmetics. We also spoke to the hair and makeup folks and they all have alibis."

Cross another idea off the list. "Oh, well. It was worth a mention. You should also know that Adrian said he was with Kristoff during the time of the murder, but he wasn't."

He held up a hand. "Got that. Kristoff was with Ashley in the master bedroom and we managed to nail down Adrian's whereabouts."

"That's good, I guess."

Someone shoved me from behind. If I didn't do something soon, a fight was going to break out.

The sheriff moved to stand in front of me and whistled. "Listen up, folks. This fine woman is off limits to you, understand? Now go about your business. I'm sure you have better things to do than harass her."

A few admirers left, but the rest decided to be stubborn and stick around.

"I'm glad it's only a spell, Rose. I'll be honest, I don't like the way they're eyeing you."

"Like a piece of meat?"

His expression darkened. "Like you belong to them."

How about that? A whiff of jealousy from the perfectly behaved Granger Nash.

"Doesn't matter how they're eyeing me when I'm not interested in any of them."

His brow lifted. "Not even the one with the biceps?"

"Pretty sure they all have biceps."

"Not as well-defined as that minotaur's."

I smiled. "If I recall correctly, yours are pretty impressive." I immediately wished I could snatch back the compliment. It didn't seem right to flirt with him. I didn't deserve to reap the benefits of our delightful banter, not after breaking his heart.

"You don't have to butter me up, Rose. I'll help you anyway." He frowned. "If I knew how to undo a spell, that is."

"Step aside, wolf." A familiar witch breezed past the crowd toward us. I felt like Frodo being rescued by Gandalf, if the white wizard had curly red hair and a face with enough makeup to open her own branch of Sephora. Her cherry red lipstick was smeared, making her appear slightly deranged—which was fairly accurate.

"Hazel, what are you doing here?"

The crazed clown looked at me askance. "What do you think? I heard you needed help."

The sheriff nodded toward my admirers. "I think I'll handle crowd control while you two deal with the magical side of things."

I squinted at Hazel. "You heard I needed help and you jumped at the chance?" That didn't sound like the Hazel I knew and avoided.

She dusted imaginary lint from her sleeve. "We Silver Moon witches stick together."

"Since when? Aunt Hyacinth said jump and you said 'sayonara, Ember.'"

Hazel ignored my response. "Just because you weren't my best student doesn't mean I'll hold it against you during a crisis."

I glanced at the gathered group of attractive paranormals. "I'd hardly consider this a crisis."

Hazel relaxed her shoulders and groaned. "Should I step out for a minute and let your ego be boosted?"

"No, no. It's fine," I said in mock resignation. "I get the opportunity to be adored all the time."

"Darn right you do. You're just too numb-skulled to notice." Hazel inclined her head toward the sheriff, who was dealing with crowd control.

My cheeks started to burn from embarrassment. "I'm not oblivious."

She dropped her bottomless satchel to the floor and began rifling through it. "I should have what we need to undo the enchantment."

"How did you find me here?" I pictured someone shining a spotlight in the sky. Instead of the Bat signal, it

Magic & Marriage

was the silhouette of a witch falling off a broomstick or hanging off the curve of a half moon by her fingertips.

"There was a phone chain."

Less exciting than a Bat signal but equally effective, apparently.

"It was supposed to be Wren's turn, but he's stuck in line at the hardware store. They're training a new cashier and it's as slow as a turtle going uphill."

"I appreciate you taking his place."

She shrugged. "No choice. I was next on the list. How do you manage to get yourself into these messes?" she grumbled.

"Raoul was only trying to help."

Her brow creased as she looked up at me. "The raccoon did this?"

"He's not just a raccoon. He's my familiar."

"I know, but still." Shaking her head, she muttered to herself.

"What?"

"I'm impressed, that's all." She produced a spool of white thread from the bag, as well as a cinnamon stick and a packet of matches.

"That's an interesting assortment." At least the cinnamon would produce a pleasant aroma while she undid the spell. Small favors.

"I need the charm."

I placed the root in her hand and she studied it for a moment. "Nice craftsmanship."

"Next thing you know, you'll be enrolling him in the University of Scribbles."

"Not going to happen." Hazel wiggled her fingers. "No opposable thumbs make writing difficult."

"Ember, are you nearly finished?" one of the men called.

"I'm pining worse than Adonis. I'll end up on the bank of your river for eternity."

"You seem to have Adonis confused with Narcissus," Hazel snapped. She turned back to me and shook her head. "I'd need an educated one or it's not going to work."

I bit back a smile. Hazel was even picky about her imaginary boyfriends.

She wrapped the white thread around the root until the red thread was no longer visible. Then she tucked the cinnamon stick between strands.

"And now we light it on fire?"

She struck a match and handed it to me. "Yes, but you must do the honors. Light the end of the stick."

"Without burning one of us?" There was a reason I never picked up smoking as a teenager and it wasn't because of the health warnings.

"It's magic, you ninny. It'll be fine."

"Ember, I love you! I want us to be together until our corpses rot side by side."

Lovely. I took the burning match and lit the stick. The smell of cinnamon intensified. I watched as the haze of love seemed to dissipate from their eyes until the fire stopped burning. One by one they returned to normal, sneaking a confused glance at me before wandering away without a word. Only the minotaur with the biceps walked over to give me a last look.

"You want to have dinner sometime?" he asked.

"What's your name?"

"Cody. I'm a personal trainer."

"It's nice to meet you, Cody, but I think you'd be wasting your time."

"No problem. I figured it was a worth a shot." He aimed

his fingers at me like a gun and made a clicking sound before sauntering away.

"See?" Hazel said. "It wasn't the charm in his case."

"I have a feeling Cody plays a numbers game. Ask enough women and you'll get enough dates."

Hazel cast me a sidelong glance. "And why would a guy built like that be wasting his time with you?"

I straightened. "Because of Sheridan, of course. I'm smitten."

"Right. Sheridan Sinclair, the television hunk and heir to a small fortune." She packed up her bag and slung the strap over her shoulder. "It was good to see you again, Ember. Let's not make a habit of it."

"Don't intend to."

"Is it true Hyacinth doesn't know about the show filming in her house?"

I stiffened. "Where did you hear that?"

She sucked in a breath. "Great Goddess, would I love to be a fly on the wall when she gets back."

"About that...do you happen to know where she went?"

She looked at me slyly. "Didn't she tell you?"

"Hard to tell someone you're technically not speaking to."

"Didn't she tell Florian?"

"She told him one thing, then apparently did another."

"Then why ask me if you already know?"

Because something told me it wasn't the truth. Aunt Hyacinth rarely traveled outside Starry Hollow and it seemed odd that she'd take a trip by herself. Who was carrying her bags?

"Forget I asked." I motioned to the satchel. "Thanks for saving me. You didn't have to do that."

Hazel lifted her chin a fraction. "Like I said, we look out for our own."

"Except when the leader of your own tells you not to."

Her cheeks reddened slightly. "Good luck with the competition. I hope it works out the way you want it to." The red-haired witch pivoted to face the door and marched out of the room.

"Well, that was unexpected," I mumbled.

Behind the counter, the barista held up a large coffee cup. "This is for you. I added a shot of Go Away and Leave Me Alone. On the house."

I hurried to the counter. "Thanks, you're the best. I didn't even know that shot was an option."

She wore a wry smile. "It is now. I just invented it. Maybe you can order it the next time you come in, to be on the safe side."

I took an indulgent sip. "I appreciate the concern, but I think the situation's been resolved." Although I made a mental note to order it the next time I was likely to see Aunt Hyacinth.

I turned toward the door, hoping to see the sheriff so I could thank him for his help, but the werewolf was already gone.

16

I arrived home to find Raoul in the kitchen with his paw in a box of cereal. "Why are you eating out of the cereal box at this hour?"

Raoul looked up from the cereal box. *I'm depressed.*

"You could distract yourself by rubbing my feet." I sat on a chair and kicked off my shoes.

The raccoon looked at my bare feet. *I already said I'm depressed. Are you trying to make me suicidal?*

"Just FYI, I don't recommend your pocket charm to make progress with Fancy Nancy."

He climbed on the chair beside me. *That bad, huh?*

"Hazel had to rescue me from an unruly mob."

How unruly? Like they refused to stand in a straight line or are we talking pitchforks?

I reached into the cereal box and took a few pieces. "Does it matter?"

I've given up on Fancy Nancy.

"Why? She's pretty," I said. And a little dramatic, but I kept that part to myself.

Raoul exhaled. *I know.*

"What's the problem? You seemed so smitten."

I am. That's the problem. I think she's just using me to get close to Thornhold.

"Why would she want to do that?" Thornhold already had a resident cat and Precious was not to be trifled with. She was my aunt's familiar through and through.

I don't know. She's so hard to read.

"I'm sorry."

It's okay. She licked me, so there's that.

"How nice for you."

Want to know where?

I winced. "Why on earth would I want to know that?"

He sniffed. *Get your mind out of the trash heap, Ember. Not where on me. Where it happened.*

Oh. "Where did it happen?"

In the moonlight, under a canopy of stars. It was the most romantic moment of my life. He clutched his furry chest. *But I knew it wasn't meant to be. The lack of communication would be a problem.*

"Always," I agreed.

The sound of the front door opening and closing signaled Marley's arrival from school. I left the kitchen and entered the living room to greet her. A taller girl stood beside her, wearing the same uniform. Her short hair was dyed green and her nose was pierced with a small gemstone.

"You must be Jinx." I'd completely forgotten about my offer to have Marley's friend over.

"It's nice to meet you, Mrs...Miss Rose?"

"Ember's fine." I pivoted to Marley. "How was school?"

She dropped her backpack on the floor with a heavy thud. "Good. The author visit went well." Marley gave me a meaningful look.

"Did you speak to him?"

She shook her head.

Jinx seemed to grasp the exchange because she said, "I was there. I'm taller, so Marley sat behind me. He seemed kind of stiff, to be honest."

"It's his way," Marley said, somewhat defensively.

I stroked her hair. "I'm glad it worked out."

Bonkers swooped into the room, from where I had no idea. Someone must've opened a window—and by someone, I meant Raoul.

The winged black cat landed on Marley's shoulder.

Jinx's eyes danced with delight. "She's amazing. Can I hold her?"

Marley tilted her head to consult her familiar. "Bonkers says if it's okay with me, then it's okay with her."

"Cool." Jinx darted forward. The moment her hands touched the cat's fur, Bonkers hissed. Jinx quickly withdrew.

"Bonkers," Marley scolded her. "That's rude."

"I thought you said she was fine with it." Jinx shook her hand as though she'd actually been bitten.

Bonkers took flight.

"I bet she's jealous," Jinx said. "Familiars can be territorial when it comes to their witch."

"What about your familiar?" Marley asked.

Jinx shrugged. "Ebony's not as cool as yours. She doesn't fly." Her gaze flicked to me. "Is yours really a raccoon?"

"The rumors are true. He's in the kitchen eating out of the cereal box, or he was a few minutes ago."

My phone buzzed with a message from Adrian. I was beginning to think they'd failed to find another place to film.

Whitethorn. 1 hour. Dressy casual.

"Duty calls," I announced. "Let me see if Mrs. Babcock is around."

Marley grimaced. "Mom, we don't need Mrs. Babcock. We're not babies."

"My parents leave me alone all the time to go out with their friends," Jinx chimed in.

I observed the two girls. "Are you sure your parents won't mind you hanging out here while I'm gone? It could run late."

Jinx plucked her phone off the table and tapped the screen. "Ask them yourself." She pressed the speaker button. "Hey, Mom. Ms. Rose…Ember wants to know if I can keep Marley company while she goes out. Is that cool with you?"

"Of course. Tell her you're very responsible and we trust you."

Well, that was nice. And unusual. I mean, I trusted Marley but I considered us to be an anomaly. Maybe we weren't as different as I believed.

"She can sleep over, right?" Marley added.

Sneaky little devil, putting me on the spot. Still, it made sense under the circumstances.

"Sure, why not?"

"Fern, you don't have your toothbrush or anything," her mother lamented.

"I'll be fine. It'll be like camping."

"We have a spare toothbrush," I said.

"If you're sure you don't mind…" her mother said.

"It'll be good to have someone to keep Marley company."

"Then I guess we'll see you in the morning, Fern. Have fun!"

I waved at the phone like a moron. It wasn't like she could see me.

Jinx gave me a smug look and set her phone on the table. Teenagers.

"I'll try not to be too late," I told the girls.

Marley removed her cloak and hung it on the coat rack. "Relax, Mom. It isn't a school night. We can sleep in if we're up late."

"I sleep in even if I'm not up late," Jinx added.

Again, teenagers.

"Okay, but if you run into a problem, call Aster or Linnea."

Marley patted her phone. "I have them on speed dial."

"We're badass witches," Jinx said. "If there's a problem, we can handle it ourselves."

Marley nodded in agreement.

I decided not to argue. The odds of anything happening were slim and I didn't want to give Marley's anxiety a boost.

I ran upstairs to find something that qualified as dressy casual and chose a cobalt blue top with a boatneck and black trousers. I drew the line at heels. I didn't bother with makeup, knowing I'd be attacked by Delilah and her brushes anyway.

As I drove to the Whitethorn, I wondered what the competition would be tonight. I was glad I'd gotten rid of the love charm before now or the entire pub would've been at risk of falling under my spell. I would've been eliminated for sure.

The door was ajar when I arrived. I ducked through the doorway and ran into Jackie, who was gazing at the interior of the pub in awe. "This place is amazing. It looks like something out of *The Hobbit*."

For once, Jackie and I were in agreement.

"Yar! Welcome to my humble abode." Captain Duncan Yellowjacket saluted the cast and crew as they set up. His parrot companion nearly fell off his perch at the sight of the women in their asset-revealing outfits. Bittersteel was a bit of a ladies' bird.

"A vampire pirate?" Jackie whispered.

Kristoff surveyed the room and tipped back his beanie to admire the wooden beams of the ceiling. "The options in this town are endless. I wish we'd planned to rotate locations from the start. Staying at the house would've been a waste."

"So much history and charm here," Adrian agreed.

"Oh, I can tell you all about the history of this place," Captain Yellowjacket began.

"I'd love to hear more," Adrian said. "Can we have pitchers for the crew?"

"Coming right up." Captain Yellowjacket set to work pulling pints. "And I have your champagne, miss."

"Me?" Jackie asked.

"Aye." He nodded to the flute sitting on the counter.

"Did you request champagne?" I asked.

Jackie plucked a flute from the counter. "I never turn down free booze."

I hadn't been planning to drink, but one glass wouldn't hurt anything. "I'll have a glass, too, Duncan."

He set a few pitchers on the counter and poured me a glass of champagne. "Will I be famous?"

"You won't be on camera," Adrian explained, as he filled a pint glass from the pitcher. "Only Sheridan and the women."

"Lucky guy," the vampire pirate mumbled.

Bittersteel squawked. "I'll take the leftovers."

"I'm not a meal," Jackie objected.

"No, but you're definitely a snack," the parrot shot back.

Jackie smiled and sipped her champagne.

The lights came on and instructions were given. Tonight's theme was heredity. Sheridan talked about traits he'd inherited from each parent and what he'd like to pass down to the next generation. I wanted to shake him and tell him we had no control over whether we passed down blue eyes or an athletic build any more than we could control the weather. Okay, I *could* control the weather under certain circumstances, so that probably wasn't the greatest analogy.

"Now I'd like each of you to share what you feel are your best assets," Sheridan said. "Gifts that we might pass along to our future children."

I wanted to gag. Sheridan was walking in his grandmother's shoes, no doubt about it. I was tempted to tell her to relax because Sheridan wasn't going to find anybody with the right credentials in this crowd. Her pompous fears were unfounded.

Jackie didn't seem to understand the assignment because she launched into a speech about how she hoped to pass down her zest for life, which some paranormals mistook for craziness but really it was passion.

"If there's a stallion, I'm going to mount it no matter how wild it is," Jackie said, finishing her longwinded answer.

"No doubt," Daisy murmured.

"And this champagne tasted bitter," Jackie told Captain Yellowjacket. "Can I get a different brand next time?"

I peered into my glass. Mine tasted fine.

Sheridan fixed his attention on Daisy next.

"I can't offer you a grand pedigree or a bank account with more than four digits," she said, "but I have a good heart and I think that's the kind of thing that can be inherited, that the world needs more of. Goodness."

One of the women made a gagging sound. I was pretty sure it was Alyx.

"You can never have too much goodness in the world," Sheridan agreed.

"I also make an excellent lasagna, a recipe I inherited from my grandmother," Daisy finished.

"I love lasagna," Sheridan said, beaming at her. He sounded sincere, although it was hard to tell. He seemed willing to say anything to get into these women's pants. He didn't even have to say anything particularly clever. Oh, to be a sought-after bachelor on television. The world was his oyster and he was happy to suck it dry.

I happened to glance at Jackie, whose skin had turned ghostly pale. "Jackie, are you okay?"

"I...don't feel well." Her body stiffened. The empty flute slid from her hand and landed on top of my shoe. I shifted to set my glass on the counter and let the flute roll to the floor.

Jackie started to seize and fell to the floor.

"Jackie!" I crouched beside her.

Sheridan rushed forward and Jackie vomited all over his expensive loafers.

"He's not going to choose her tonight," Alyx said in a stage whisper.

Sheridan stared at his shoes in disbelief.

"Somebody bring a rag and a mop!" Adrian shouted.

I turned Jackie on her side and smoothed back her hair as she continued to convulse. "It's okay. You're going to be okay." I turned to the crowd. "I think we need an ambulance."

"I'm a healer," someone shouted. "Let me through."

I glanced up at the unfamiliar druid. "Are you part of the production?"

Magic & Marriage

"No, I'm on vacation." She nudged me aside. "But I haven't had a drink yet, so I can help her."

I watched as the druid worked her hands over Jackie's body. "I sense poison," she said. "I need to withdraw it from her system."

"Give her space," Bittersteel squawked. The parrot flew in front of the encroaching crowd to encourage them to back up.

I remained on the floor with Jackie and held her hand while the druid worked. Her eyes were closed most of the time and I could only imagine the intense concentration required to remove poison from a body. I glanced at the empty flute on the floor and snatched it. I gave it a sniff. I didn't smell anything out of the ordinary.

"She'll survive," the healer finally said.

My hands shook from relief. "It's lucky you were here."

"I nearly wasn't. The owner said they could only allow a few extra patrons tonight on account of the production and we had to stay over there." She waved a hand to the far side of the room. "I only got a seat because another woman left."

I glanced at Jackie, who looked far less crazy with her eyes closed. "Can you tell what kind of poison it was?"

"I think so, but it's not an exact science. For that, we'd need...science."

"Was it strychnine?"

Her eyes rounded. "How did you know?"

"Because it's the same substance used to poison someone else in the competition."

The healer cringed. "When did dating become such a dangerous activity?"

"Looks like Jackie's out," Adrian said, looming over us and shaking his head.

"No offense to Jackie, but I wasn't going to choose her

anyway," Sheridan said. "I was planning to send her packing after what she said at Haverford House."

The news didn't surprise me. I figured he was biding his time until the next ceremony to get rid of her.

"We can't leave her here to recover," I said.

"Already on it."

I looked up at Sheriff Nash. "I didn't know you were here."

"I wasn't. Duncan called me."

A team entered the room with a stretcher and shifted Jackie onto it. I watched them whisk her out of the pub.

I turned to the sheriff and gave him the flute in my hand. "You might want this. I think it's evidence."

He wrapped the flute in a white cloth and tucked it into his pocket. "Any thoughts on what happened, Rose?"

"The killer is seriously misguided if they think Jackie had a chance of winning."

"Maybe the poison was intended for someone else. How were the glasses distributed?"

I felt a pair of eyes burning into my back. "Let's table this conversation for later."

I moved away from the sheriff and casually turned to see who'd been watching me. Daisy. It was only when I looked more closely that I noticed the tears shining in her eyes.

"You're upset about Jackie," I said.

"Tish. Jackie. This is only a show. It isn't worth all this pain and suffering."

Sheridan overheard her. "You can't quit now. You've made it this far."

Daisy tilted her chin to address him. "I didn't say anything about quitting. I only wish this production hadn't become such a danger zone. It's..." She hesitated, seeming to

Magic & Marriage

want to choose her next words carefully. "It's pointless and unnecessary."

Adrian clapped her on the back. "That's television, sweetheart. Pointless and unnecessary."

At least Daisy seemed to have a heart and a conscience, which was more than I could say for most of the participants. The other women were milling around the pub like someone had tripped over a loose floorboard rather than narrowly avoided death from poison.

I thought about the sheriff's question as to whether the glass might have been intended for someone else. I shot him a text. *Meet me on the rooftop in five.*

No one else here would know about the access point to the rooftop and Duncan wouldn't tell them. Once I was certain everyone's attention was elsewhere, I slipped through a 'staff only' door and found the creaky wooden staircase that took me to the roof of the ancient building. Hugging myself to stave off the nighttime chill, I observed the dark, choppy water as I waited for the sheriff. The moon was remarkably silver tonight. It resembled a round mirror affixed to a dark wall.

A Granger-shaped silhouette swaggered across the rooftop. "A secret rendezvous, Rose? I gotta say, I like your style."

"I didn't want to leave the room, but anywhere else risked being overheard. No one knows about the roof."

He cut through the shadows and stepped into a beam of moonlight. The effect was transformative. The warm brown eyes. The lush head of hair that itched to be touched. The biceps that begged to be squeezed. It was like I was seeing him for the first time all over again.

"Do you remember the day we met?" I asked.

"You called me away from a crime scene to reminisce?

That's not like you, Rose." A faint smile touched his lips. "But yeah, of course I remember. How could I forget? I could tell you were scared witless but you put up a good front."

I'd been a suspect in the death of the coven's Maiden, a young witch called Fleur. The sheriff had made his distaste for my family clear during that first meeting.

"I wasn't scared witless. I was very brave under the circumstances."

"I didn't say you weren't brave. What do you think bravery is but showing courage in the face of fear? You've always shown remarkable courage. One of the bravest paranormals I've ever known, in fact. It's one of the many qualities I admire about you."

"Thanks, Granger. That means a lot coming from you."

As much I wanted to hear more about my admirable qualities, I knew we couldn't linger too long or someone would notice my absence.

"I saw you talking to Duncan. Did he notice anybody near the flute?"

The sheriff shook his head. "Says the place was a madhouse and he didn't notice who ordered it, who was near it. Nothing. But he remembered the name Jackie."

"I assumed she'd ordered the champagne herself, but when I think about our conversation, I don't think she did."

"So Jackie was the target?" He rocked back and forth on his heels, mulling over the information. "You said Jackie had no chance of winning. Can you think of any other reason she might've been a target?"

"Other than she's weird and probably nuts, no."

He sank his hands deep into his pockets. "It's beautiful up here. Duncan ought to set up a table and chairs and upsell it as a romantic spot."

"But customers would have to walk through the cobwebs

and past the buckets and mops to get here," I said. "Not exactly appetizing."

"True, plus they'd be missing out on the best part."

I smiled. "A murder investigation?"

He met my gaze, unsmiling. "You wouldn't be standing here under the stars, looking like a gift from the heavens."

My heart skipped a beat. As I opened my mouth to respond, my phone rang and Evelyn Sinclair's name popped on the screen. The woman was relentless. I let the call go to voicemail. Her update could wait.

He inclined his head toward the phone. "I guess you're wanted back downstairs."

The romantic moment had passed as quickly as it had appeared. I cursed Evelyn Sinclair for her bad timing. Then again, now wasn't the time to focus on my personal life. I had a job to do—a few jobs, in fact. There was always tomorrow for us.

I hoped.

"I'll head down first. Just wait two minutes before following me."

The sheriff nodded. "I wish I could conduct all my business under these conditions. Much more appealing."

"I don't think Deputy Bolan would provide quite the same atmosphere."

"Maybe not, but it'd be too dark to see him scowling at me. I consider that a win."

Only Granger Nash could make me laugh after what happened in the pub. "I'd better get back before they notice I'm gone. Will you keep me updated on Jackie's condition?"

He nodded. "I'll head over there now to talk to her when she's able. See if she noticed anything." He opened his mouth as if to say more, but seemed to think better of it. "Take care of yourself, Rose."

I squeezed his arm. "You don't have to worry about me."

"Maybe not, but I still do."

I forced myself to exit the rooftop and return to Sheridan and the rest of the cast and crew. Although my head was in the pub answering inane questions about heredity, I'd left my heart on the rooftop under the watchful eye of a silver moon.

17

I woke up early enough the next morning to make pancakes for Marley and Jinx. If I couldn't be around last night, the least I could do was provide them with a hearty breakfast.

As I flipped over the pancakes on the griddle, Raoul climbed through the kitchen window. *I thought I smelled something good.*

"Are you feeling any better?"

I will when I have a short stack covered in syrup. He sat on the counter and watched the pancakes turn golden.

PP3's bark pierced the air. Great timing.

"You're in charge," I told Raoul and set the spatula on the counter.

I hurried to the living room. The Yorkie stood with his nose pressed to the crack beneath the front door.

"Looks like Raoul isn't the only one with a scenting superpower."

I opened the door and immediately felt the same pulsing energy I experienced when I stumbled upon Raoul's picnic with Fancy Nancy. I glanced down at the doormat and saw the white cat.

"Meow," she said, and I detected a note of urgency.

I bent down to examine the cat. It was possible the energy wasn't coming from the cat but the pink collar. Maybe the gemstones were enchanted.

An image of Ben flashed in my mind, Myrtle's canine companion. I'd briefly entertained the notion of a young man being trapped in the form of a dog. I'd dismissed the notion, but maybe the idea wasn't without merit. Maybe this was the reason Raoul couldn't understand Fancy Nancy. It wasn't because she was a cat.

It was because she *wasn't* a cat.

Instinctively, I unbuckled the collar and let it fall to the doormat. The silky white hair dissolved and the feline face morphed into a more human one. The body stretched and the tail shrank until it disappeared. Paws became hands and feet. An elf with cornsilk hair stared at me, wide-eyed. He wore gray sweatpants and a white T-shirt. His feet were bare.

"You must be Harold," I said.

The elf stared at me, wide-eyed. "How'd you know?"

"You mow Marigold's lawn."

Harold blinked at me. "Did I not show up this week?" He scratched behind his ear. "I'm sorry about that. I can be forgetful." He turned from side to side. "Where am I? How did I get there?"

"You don't remember being a cat?"

Harold absently licked his hand. "No. Why was I a cat?"

I wasn't entirely sure. "You should call your parents. They haven't heard from you in a week." I retrieved his phone and charger from the table and delivered them to the doorstep. "Here. These are yours. Go home and take a hot shower. You've been hanging out in the garbage bins."

Magic & Marriage

Harold sniffed under his arms and nodded. "I can tell."

As Harold departed, I realized I would have to break the news to Raoul that the love of his life was actually a twenty-year-old elf named Harold who mowed lawns for a living.

"Nope," I told myself. "Not going to do it." There was no point. Raoul had already come to the conclusion that they wouldn't work as a couple. Best to let him keep his romantic memories.

Pancakes are ready, Raoul said.

I'll be there in a minute. I picked up the pink collar. It served as a good reminder that things were not always as they seemed. There'd been signs that something was amiss with the cat, but Raoul and I had been too distracted to notice. She looked and sounded like all the other cats, but all this time Fancy Nancy had harbored a secret, much like most of the women taking part in Natural Selection, except the cat's had been about her—or his identity.

A secret about identity.

"Mom, is something wrong?"

I spun around to see Marley at the bottom of the steps. "Is Jinx still asleep?"

She nodded. "What's going on? You've got that look in your eye."

"I think I may have figured out the killer."

"Please call Sheriff Nash."

I tugged my phone from my pocket. "That was my next step. There are pancakes in the kitchen."

Marley brightened. "Thanks. Jinx and I were talking last night. Would it be okay if we went shopping in town later today?"

"Sounds good. I can drop you off."

"We'd rather go by ourselves, but thanks."

Great Mother of Abraham Lincoln. She really was

growing up before my eyes. It was equally thrilling and terrifying. "Okay. There's money in the drawer by the refrigerator."

I sent a text to the sheriff. Then I ran upstairs to get dressed and fix my hair. The glamor of television must've been rubbing off on me. If we were about to catch a killer, I wanted to look my best doing it.

THE SHERIFF'S Office was quiet when I arrived. Nobody was behind the reception desk, so I ventured to the interrogation room. Sure enough, Sheriff Nash was on one side of the table.

Daisy sat on the other.

"Nice of you to join us, Rose," he said, smirking. "Stopped off for a trim and a blowout, did you?"

Daisy craned her neck to look at me. "Are you a suspect, too?"

I sat in the empty chair next to the sheriff. "Not a suspect."

"Then why are you here?"

The sheriff looked at me with a sly grin. "Yes, Rose. Why are you here?" He inclined his head. "And for that matter, why'd you ask me to bring her in? Your message was vague."

Daisy blinked in confusion. "Why would you tell the sheriff to bring me in?"

I fixed with her a hard look. "Because you may look and act like the rest of us, but you're not. You are not at all what you seem, are you?"

She shifted awkwardly in her seat. "I don't understand."

"Oh, I think you do. You're Sheridan's girlfriend. His real girlfriend."

Daisy hesitated, appearing unsure how to proceed.

Magic & Marriage

Finally, she allowed herself a tiny smile. "Busted. How did you know?"

"It took a little time, but I got there in the end." I reeled off the long list of clues. For starters, Sheridan mentioned he and Daisy only lived a few miles apart. Daisy suggested we film in Elixir because she knew the club from living here. Maybe she'd even met Sheridan there. He also didn't seem to care whether I liked him or not. At first I thought it was arrogance, but eventually I realized it was because his heart already belonged to someone else. Then Daisy was the one who voluntarily wanted to get the women together after Tish's death because she was the only one who wasn't in a cutthroat competition. She knew she'd already won.

Daisy folded her arms in a protective gesture. "I didn't kill Tish if that's what you're thinking. I had no reason to. Like you said, I know I'm going to win. Why bother to kill anyone?"

"I don't know. Jealousy. We saw a patch of Tish's pink lipstick on his cheek that first day that might have sent you over the edge."

She rolled her eyes. "If I got upset about a bit of kissing, our plan would never have worked."

"Plan?" the sheriff interrupted.

"To get married."

I shook my head. "I don't understand. Why would you need a plan to get married?"

Her face hardened. "Because of his grandmother, that tiresome beast. She would never approve of me. She thinks Sheridan walks on water. I mean, I love him more than anything, but even I know he has flaws."

"So why not stand up to her? If he loves you, shouldn't he tell her to keep her opinions to herself?"

"He can't do that. He'd risk his inheritance. We figure the

show is a way around her. Once he chooses me as his wife on the show, public opinion will be in our favor. Image is everything to the Sinclairs. She'll have no choice but to go along with it. She would rather let him marry me than endure the scandal of a broken contract."

"Then maybe you should get pregnant," I said, only half joking.

"Sheridan doesn't want his son to be born out of wedlock. He wants legitimate heirs only."

I peered at her. "His son?"

"He assumes our firstborn will be a son like all the Sinclair children." She cringed. "Gosh, I hope I don't disappoint them."

It would be nice if Sheridan could get over the whole son-and-heir thing, but he seemed to have been successfully brainwashed. "You're lucky you're not marrying King Henry or disappointment would be the least of your worries."

Daisy gave me a blank look. "Because he was obese?"

"Never mind." Apparently they didn't teach Tudor history in great detail in the paranormal world.

"Did you poison Jackie?" the sheriff asked.

She recoiled. "Absolutely not. I was horrified when that happened. Why would I do that?"

A memory flashed in my mind of Daisy's reaction to Jackie falling ill.

Tish. Jackie. This is only a show. It isn't worth all this pain and suffering. I only wish this production hadn't become such a danger zone. It's pointless and unnecessary.

It was pointless and unnecessary because she and Sheridan had known what the outcome would be. So Daisy didn't poison Jackie out of jealousy. What other reason was there to eliminate the crazy one, especially given that Sheridan had planned to send her home last night anyway?

"Can you think of any reason the producers might want Jackie to go?" The only reason to poison Jackie would be to remove her from the competition.

"The producers had to know from the start that Jackie had no chance. Her crazy was apparent from day one. Sheridan sent me a text that first night to tell me how uncomfortable she made him."

"Why did Sheridan agree to keep Bianca after she was eliminated?"

She began to pout. "We had a genuine fight over that. He swears he was trying to be convincing and that having a double date with Ashley and Bianca would make it easier to get rid of them both."

"Did you believe him?" the sheriff asked.

"I did. Honestly, I haven't been genuinely concerned about any of the women, no offense, Ember. That's why I was so surprised about Tish. Just because she stole the first kiss didn't make her a frontrunner. It was only the first day."

Her words echoed something Honey had said in the Caffeinated Cauldron. *How could they decide so quickly that Tish was the one to beat?*

What if they hadn't decided quickly? What if they believed Sheridan was already involved with Tish before production started?

"Has Sheridan mentioned whether anyone suspected he was in a relationship?" I asked. "Maybe the killer thought it was Tish because she was so forward with him so quickly."

She pursed her lips. "He hasn't mentioned anything, but you can ask him."

The theory didn't narrow down the list of suspects though. Any of the remaining women had a stake in the outcome. If the competition had a predetermined winner, that was bad for everyone except Sheridan and the chosen bride. Even the producers would be upset by that.

The producers.

Maybe not Kristoff—he was too smitten with Ashley to care about anything or anyone—but he wasn't the only one invested in the show.

The sheriff seemed to sense my thought process because he said, "The producers have alibis. Pretty much everybody has an alibi."

I looked at Daisy. "Has Sheridan mentioned anything to you about Tish? About who he thinks might have killed her?"

She shook her head. "Neither one of us has talked much about it. He knows the whole thing upsets me. If it weren't for our secret, none of this would've happened. It's our fault Tish is dead, even if we didn't poison her. And neither of us likes Jackie, but it's still awful what happened to her. She didn't deserve to be hurt like that."

No, she didn't.

Her expression turned hopeful. "Does this mean I can leave now?"

"Yes," the sheriff said. "Don't leave town."

She smiled. "Wouldn't dream of it. This is my home. This is where Sheridan and I plan to grow our family."

The sheriff and I waited until she left to exchange glances.

"This case gets more interesting by the day, Rose."

"Did you confirm her alibi?" I asked.

"I don't think she did it, do you? The question bothering me is—why poison one woman with the intent to kill but not the other?"

I shot him a quizzical look. "What do you mean? Jackie got lucky because there was a healer present."

Magic & Marriage

"She was poisoned in front of everyone. The killer had to know she'd be surrounded by the cast and crew at the time, unlike Tish. Plus the amount of strychnine in her system was less than we found in Tish's system. The killer knew how much to use to kill because they'd already done it."

"And they deliberately used less for Jackie." The sheriff was right. It sounded like the intent was to hurt Jackie rather than kill her. "But what does that tell us?"

"No idea yet, but it's sure worth thinking about."

"The list of suspects has dwindled, but I don't feel any closer to the truth."

"Yeah, for a second, I thought you might've been right about Daisy, but I can tell she regrets this whole ruse."

I glanced at the empty doorway. "To be fair, I'm glad. I like her."

He leaned back in his chair and slotted his hands behind his head. "And we don't think Sheridan has a hand in it?"

"I can't think of a motive, can you?"

He shook his head. "Deputy Pitt suggested he's a serial killer who found the ideal platform for his talents."

I stifled a laugh. "I think she might be watching too many cop shows."

"That's what Bolan told her. She's young, though. Plenty of time to learn."

I decided to ask the question I'd been avoiding. "Would you ever consider dating her?"

Two roasted chestnuts squinted at me. "You can't be serious, Rose. That's a definite no. Not even a question."

"Because of the age gap? The professional conflict?"

He snorted. "No, Rose. None of those things."

I didn't press the issue. "I'm sorry I was wrong. I'd really hoped you'd be able to make an arrest today."

He grinned. "Trying to lighten my load? That's kind of you."

"I'm your woman on the inside, right? It's my job." I rose to my feet. "I guess I'll head home then. Let me know if you hear anything."

"I think I'll have another word with Sheridan. Care to join me?"

"I'll pass. I've seen Sheridan Sinclair enough this week to last me a lifetime."

He chuckled. "Why don't you tell me how you really feel?"

I gazed at him with longing. If only. "I'll talk to you later, Granger."

I left the office without another word.

18

The cottage was empty when I returned home. Marley and Jinx were shopping. Raoul was probably at the dump looking for his next girlfriend. PP3 was asleep upstairs. I glanced at the pink collar I'd left on the table. It occurred to me I hadn't told Marigold about Harold's safe return. I sent her a quick text to let her know. She'd be happy. The elf was back just in time for the next weekly mow. I considered performing a spell on the collar to see if I could figure out who enchanted it. It would take a little research. First, a snack. Magic was hungry work.

While I was in the kitchen, I heard the front door open and close. "You're back sooner than I expected," I called to Marley.

The kitchen door swung open and Evelyn Sinclair's cane clicked across the floor. "There you are, my dear."

Wow. Talk about entitled. "I don't have an update for you, Mrs. Sinclair. Alyx won the date at the Whitethorn and I don't have any details yet about the next event."

"Sheridan never should've agreed to this ridiculous farce. He's above this sort of thing."

"But he did, which is why you chose me to interfere. By controlling the winner, you knew he wouldn't have to make good on any promise of marriage."

She sniffed. "As though I could abide any of those trollops as my granddaughter-in-law."

I leaned a hip against the counter. "You know what, Mrs. Sinclair? They're not trollops. Well, mostly. Maybe Bianca. Daisy's a lovely woman. And Leesa wants to expand her real estate business. Alyx wants to be an electrician if the acting thing doesn't work out, which I say more power to her, pun fully intended."

"And they all want to marry my Sheridan for the money. I won't have it." She slammed the bottom of her cane on the floor to punctuate the statement.

"It isn't up to you. Sheridan is a grown man who can make his own decisions. In fact, it's imperative that he does. You do him no favors by coddling him."

"A decision like that could cost this family everything."

"I think you overestimate the damage. You know, if I hadn't made a mistake when I was a teenager, I wouldn't have the best thing that ever happened to me. Mistakes can bring unexpected joy, or teach us valuable lessons. Trust me, I know. I'm an expert." I thought about Granger. "Sometimes if we're lucky, we get a do-over."

"I don't care if these floozies all want to be president, they're not good enough for my Sheridan."

"I've got news for you, Mrs. Sinclair, your beloved Sheridan isn't so special. Even Clementine knew it the moment she met him."

She narrowed her eyes. "Which one is Clementine?"

I laughed at her overblown reaction. "She's a cat."

"You say another disparaging word about my grandson and I won't pay you the remainder of the bill."

I stared at her for a moment, debating my options. I needed the money. On the other hand, she'd basically dared me.

"Sheridan Sinclair is so small, he's basically a eunuch."

She gasped and recoiled. "I don't even know what that means."

I shook my head. "It's a playground insult. I have a lot of experience with those."

"Two can play at that game." Mrs. Sinclair surveyed the kitchen. "Your kitchen looks like it belongs to a servant. Your taste isn't anywhere near the level of your aunt's." Her gaze landed on the stovetop. "I must say it's the first time I've seen a kettle quite so grand. A mahogany handle and whistle. Looked like a piece of art. Your kettle looks as though it was rescued from the garbage heap."

An unfavorable comparison to Aunt Hyacinth? Did she really think that would...? My thoughts faltered. Something nagged at me, but I couldn't put my finger on it.

"What is it, my dear?" She tapped her cane on the floor. "Ah, let me guess. You've begun to regret your decision to insult my grandson. I can hardly blame you."

"He's nice enough, but he's not my type." Although seeing Sheridan through Daisy's eyes made me like him a little bit more. There certainly seemed to be more depth to him than I'd gleaned. It also meant that a lot of what he'd said to me during our date was probably for the benefit of the show, to put me off.

"He's every woman's type. It's the women who are lacking."

Poor Daisy. She might tick the Natural Selection boxes in the eyes of the audience, but definitely not in the eyes of his grandmother.

Sweet. Baby. Elvis.

My heart slammed into my chest as the pieces fell into place. "You were in my aunt's kitchen the first day of filming."

"I stopped by to see how things had gone. I check in with Sheridan every day."

My fingers inched across the counter to reach my phone. "Tell me, Mrs. Sinclair. How long have you known about Daisy?"

The matriarch didn't even flinch. "I told you when I hired you that I was willing to do whatever it takes to prevent my grandson from making a grave error in judgment."

"You found out that first day of filming, didn't you?" If she'd known from the outset, there would have been no reason to hire me. She must've discovered it afterward and acted quickly.

"I discovered his treachery at Thornhold, yes. I overheard him on the phone, assuring someone their plan would work."

"And you really thought killing an innocent woman was preferable to letting him marry the woman he loves?"

"I didn't intend to kill an innocent woman. I intended to kill Daisy. I assumed from the woman's possessive behavior during filming that she was the girlfriend. Clearly, I was mistaken."

"The only thing Daisy is guilty of is falling in love with someone with a warped family."

Like my mother. She'd fallen in love with a Rose. It couldn't have been easy for her to contend with Aunt Hyacinth's antics. It was only after she died that my father finally decided to break away from the family and whisk me away to a normal life in Maple Shade, New Jersey.

"That woman is not marrying into my family. Not today. Not ever," she thundered.

"I don't think that's for you to say, Mrs. Sinclair. It'll be hard to persuade anyone to listen to you from the inside of a prison cell."

She jerked up her chin and sniffed. "I'm a Sinclair, my dear. I won't spend a single minute in prison."

"I don't know how you expect to avoid it. I know you killed Tish and you tried to kill Jackie."

"I didn't try to kill her, only put her in her place. She was rude to my grandson," the nymph snarled.

One crazy meets another, apparently.

"You ordered the champagne at the Whitethorn."

"It was such a zoo in that wretched place. No one even noticed me. I snuck out and another woman took my place inside."

"Do you seriously believe I won't turn you in?"

Her expression shifted. "No. I don't believe that at all. I'm an old woman, Ms. Rose. Do you know what that means?"

"You wish you would've moisturized more in your younger years? Slept with more men?" I paused. "Maybe a woman?"

She ignored my response. "It means I have nothing left to lose."

She stared me down with the weight of the entire Sinclair dynasty. I met the challenge, fully invoking the legacy of the One True Witch.

"I'm a Rose, lady. You think you can level me with a snooty look? Trust me. My ancestors perfected the art of superiority."

Her lips peeled away from her teeth and formed an unnerving smile. All my hackles went up. She had an ace up her sleeve. I knew it the way I knew when I was going to wake up the next morning with a zit on my chin.

"I'm not concerned about your ancestral power," she said. "You see, my dear, as always, I came prepared."

Before I could react, she raised the cane and tiny darts shot from the base, one after the other. They pierced the skin of my arm and leg. My limbs immediately began to burn. Wincing, I plucked the darts from their targets and tossed them to the floor.

"Did Sheridan mention his grandfather was a skilled inventor?"

"He said something about the family talent." The burning turned to a tingle and worked its way to my stomach and throat. "Is this the same poison you used on Tish and Jackie?"

Her smile widened and her eyes flashed with pride. "It is. It's widely available, of course, which makes it difficult to trace to any one paranormal."

The kitchen door flew open, shocking both of us. I'd recognize that kaftan-ed silhouette anywhere.

"How dare you step foot onto my property and threaten my family?" Aunt Hyacinth's voice was injected with enough venom to level an island of giants.

Mrs. Sinclair pivoted toward her, still leaning on her cane. "I assure you it was not a threat."

"Then I'm glad we understand each other."

The nymph's eyes narrowed. "It isn't a threat because the deed is done."

Aunt Hyacinth shot me a quizzical look. As if on cue, I collapsed on the floor in a heap. Although I was conscious, I was no longer in control of my body.

"Ember!"

I heard the fear in her voice as the seizure took hold. I

would've felt pleased if I were capable of feeling anything at all.

I pried open my lips to respond but no sound came out.

Aunt Hyacinth turned toward my attacker with the fury of a thousand witches burning in her eyes. "You will pay for this." There was no mistaking the tone. My aunt was out for blood.

Mrs. Sinclair whipped her cane in the air. Unlike me, my aunt was ready for her. Aunt Hyacinth flicked two fingers to the side and the cane blew from the nymph's shaky hand. As soon as it hit the floor, PP3 made a beeline to retrieve it. The dog clenched the cane in his mouth and dragged it toward my aunt. I wasn't sure when he joined the party, but I was glad to see him.

"The murder weapon will help convict you," Aunt Hyacinth said, taking control of the cane.

Mrs. Sinclair glanced at me on the floor and shrugged. "In for a penny, in for a pound."

"Tell me how to save her," my aunt demanded.

The nymph's smile remained intact. "It's too late."

"Nonsense." Aunt Hyacinth focused her full attention on the nymph. Energy crackled in the air. If she wasn't a murderous snob, I'd feel sorry for Evelyn Sinclair right now.

The nymph jerked up her chin. "Face it, Hyacinth. The almighty Roses have finally fallen."

"Never!" My aunt threw out her hands and pushed. "Retrorsus!"

Mrs. Sinclair blew backward and hit the base of her skull on a shelf. She dropped to the floor like a bag of bones. My aunt strode toward her, the pale pink fabric of the unicorn kaftan swishing around her ankles as she walked. She loomed over the barely conscious nymph. I struggled to keep my eyes open.

"Tell me what you gave her or you won't live to regret it," she ordered.

I tried to form words, to tell my aunt that it was strychnine, but only foam filtered through my lips.

The nymph looked up at my aunt with a defiant expression. "As I said, I have nothing left to lose."

"Then you've completely forgotten about your legacy. How do you think the Sinclair name will suffer as a result of your actions? Save my niece and preserve the remaining shred of your humanity."

Mrs. Sinclair twisted to look at me. "You think she's worth it? She's not a Rose in the true sense. She's nothing but a basic witch."

Aunt Hyacinth's face contorted with rage. "She's my family."

Magic exploded from her.

My body relaxed as the seizure subsided. I was able to squeeze my eyes shut to avoid the bright white flare that illuminated the room. I was almost afraid to open them again and survey the damage. Was Evelyn alive?

"Ember, I need you to do something for me." My aunt's voice was surprisingly calm and cool under the circumstances.

I tried to focus on her face, but I had trouble keeping my eyes open. A healer wouldn't make it in time to save me. I was as good as dead.

She gripped my hand. "I need you to swap bodies with me."

Did she suggest swapping bodies? Why would she want to inhabit a body on the verge of death?

"You're more powerful thanks to Ivy's magic," my aunt continued, "but I have more experience. I might be able to expel the poison."

"Strychnine," I whispered.

"Strychnine. Are you certain?"

I nodded. "What…if…can't?"

Gazing into my eyes, her expression softened. "Then I die and you live the rest of your life in my body. Not ideal, I agree."

Part of me worried this was some ploy to gain control of Ivy's power while inhabiting my body. I wouldn't put it past Aunt Hyacinth to take advantage of my vulnerable state. I had to risk it though. I had Marley to consider. The situation was too dire to ignore.

"You want to live, don't you? Raise that gorgeous daughter of yours and watch her grow into her potential?"

I nodded. Yes, I most definitely did.

"As do I. Now summon your strength and switch with me."

My vision was beginning to blur. I decided to trust her. I ignored the deterioration and concentrated on the magic inside me. I willed myself out of my body. If this worked, I swore I'd never refer to Marigold's lessons as a lost art again.

I felt a click and everything went black. If we were successful, it wasn't obvious. I couldn't see or hear anything. It was as though I was falling down a dark well. My mind began to flip through a series of unfamiliar images. I recognized my father's younger self in one of them. He delivered a plate to me. Chocolate mousse? I turned away, refusing the offering.

I seemed to be experiencing Aunt Hyacinth's memories.

"I'm sorry, Father. I tried my best."

"If that's your best, then I'm even more disappointed. Are you or are you not a Rose, Hyacinth?"

Emotional waves washed over me as more of Hyacinth's memories surfaced. Disappointment. Frustration. Anger.

Resentment. No wonder she'd become such a bitter old witch. The pressure her family put on her as a child was horrific. And pitting her against my father was despicable.

"You are the descendant of the One True Witch. You have a legacy to uphold."

"If you're not the best, then what are you? Nothing, that's what."

Her parents hurled insult after insult. Challenge after challenge. Parents were supposed to be a child's safe space, but my aunt had been far from comforted by hers. Thanks to her memories, I understood my father's escape now more than ever. He hadn't simply run away from his sister. He'd escaped from the life of being a Rose in Starry Hollow. The expectations. The demands.

There was no unconditional love. As a child, she felt powerless and, therefore, loveless. My aunt had to prove she was worthy of her parents' love by becoming powerful. She had to earn their love and respect with each and every spell until she learned to equate power with love and forgot that one had absolutely nothing to do with the other.

Being Hyacinth Rose-Muldoon wasn't easy and glamorous.

It was awful.

I shoved aside the onslaught of memories and forced my eyes open. I was greeted with a vision of myself writhing on the floor. The real me. Ember. Whatever my aunt was attempting to do to expel the poison wasn't working. I crawled across the floor and took my...her hand.

"I'm here. What do you need me to do?" It felt so strange to observe myself from another body. I spotted a freckle on my jawline that I'd never noticed before.

She struggled to look at me. Her forehead glistened from exertion. "Not...working."

My heart thumped hard against my chest. I didn't want to give this body a heart attack. I focused on my breathing and tried to calm myself. I took my phone from the pocket of the pants on the floor in front of me.

I heard my aunt's voice emanate from me as I spoke into the phone. "Send help to Rose Cottage. I've been...Ember's been poisoned and she's on the verge of death."

And then my final words.

"Please hurry."

The spell was a mistake. I couldn't let her die instead of me. It wasn't fair. I was the one who baited the killer, not Aunt Hyacinth. I had to put myself back in my body and accept the outcome.

"I'm going to swap us back," I told her.

"No." The reply was quiet but terse.

"I have to. You can't sacrifice yourself for me. It isn't right."

"Is."

"You stubborn cow. I won't let you." I was powerful enough to push her out, especially now that she'd been weakened in my body. I had to concentrate and exert my will. I was a Rose. A descendant of the One True Witch and Ivy's heir apparent.

I could do this.

I sat on the floor beside her and held her hand. Closing my eyes, I focused on my will and pushed open a metaphorical door. My effort was met with little resistance. I used my magic like a crowbar and pried the gap wide enough for me to slip inside and evict the older witch.

I felt a *snap!* sensation and knew it had worked. I was fully back in my body, which meant Aunt Hyacinth was back in hers.

Magic surged through my veins. I felt stronger somehow.

Like my time in Aunt Hyacinth's body had given me the tools I needed to kick this poison's butt. Although I couldn't identify the power by name, I knew in my gut it was what I needed to survive. She'd called forth the right magic. I only had to use it.

I conjured a memory of the healer in the Whitethorn, the one who saved Jackie, and I mimicked her movements from the inside out.

"Ember, how could you?" My aunt sounded displeased by the turn of events. I couldn't worry about her. I had to stay focused on the poison.

I identified the location of the poison in my blood, liver, kidney, and stomach wall and tried to isolate it to keep it from spreading further. The exertion took a toll.

"You can do this, Ember," my aunt said in a stern voice. "You *must*."

But I couldn't. The poison continued to spread.

Like an ear-splitting lullaby, the sound of a wailing siren accompanied me to sleep.

19

Despite the attempt at a magical purge and the healer that arrived at Rose Cottage, it still took three days to recover from the poison Mrs. Sinclair had injected into my system. If only someone had found Tish in time, she, too, might've survived. I was lucky that Aunt Hyacinth arrived when she did. I still found it hard to believe the witch had been willing to sacrifice herself for me.

Marley looked after me before and after school. Florian, Aster, Sterling, and Linnea took turns during the day and at night after Marley went to bed. Marley had even read me a brief message from Alec to say he heard the news and wished me a speedy recovery. It was a nice gesture. I wasn't sure whether he and I would ever truly be friends—too much troubled water under the bridge—but we would always care deeply about each other. Some bonds could never be broken.

On the subject of unbreakable bonds, Granger sent flowers and asked me if he could come by to wrap up the final details of the case once I was feeling up to it. Now that I was capable of showering and making myself presentable, I invited him for dinner.

Are you cooking? Granger texted.

Do I look crazy to you?

Only around the eyes. See you at seven, nutball, he replied.

The sound of the doorbell startled me. I swung my legs over the side of the bed and headed downstairs. Marigold stood in the living room, looking contrite.

"I'm glad to see you up and around," she said.

I folded my arms. "I take it you're here to pay me my fee —and apologize."

She produced a check from her purse and set it on the table. "Yes, your fee. I figure you'll need the money since you've been out of commission for a few days."

I kept my arms folded and continued to glare at her. "Still waiting on that apology."

Her gaze darted to the door, as though trying to judge how quickly she could escape. "I don't know what you mean."

She raced for the door and I used magic to lock it. "I think you do. You see, I've had a lot of time to think while I've been bedridden."

The witch turned to face me and leaned against the door. "It was an accident. I was working on a spell and Harold was in the wrong place at the wrong time."

I didn't buy her story for a single second.

"There's no Myrtle, is there? You made up the soup story."

Marigold gave me a sheepish look. "There is a Myrtle. She just isn't as I described."

"No, she isn't. She's a wonderful fairy and I'm glad to have met her."

She beamed at me. "See? Result!" She spun around and jiggled the door handle. Still locked.

"What did you do?" I pressed. "Show up on his doorstep and turn him into a cat?" That would explain why his phone was still at the apartment.

She twisted to look at me. "Pretty much."

"You spelled an innocent elf for the sole purpose of letting me find him? What kind of whack-a-doodle nonsense is that?"

"I was already peeved with him. He hadn't been turning up to mow and my lawn started to look like I'd been playing Jumanji in the garden."

"So you decided to teach him a lesson and let me play detective at the same time?"

She patted the sides of my shoulders. "Well done. You cracked the case. I never doubted it for a minute."

I smacked her hand away. "You're paying me to find someone when you knew all along where he was."

"Not technically. I mean, I knew I'd turned him into a cat, but I didn't expect him to take off. I had no idea where he was."

"Then why not hang up flyers?"

"I didn't have a picture now, did I? He wasn't really my cat. Besides, I wanted it to be suitably challenging for you."

I gaped at her. "You told me it wasn't a pity job."

Closing her eyes, she rubbed her lips together. "I lied. I'm sorry."

"I'm not desperate, Marigold. I'm perfectly capable of landing real clients who genuinely need my help. What you did was insulting, not to mention dangerous."

Marigold stared at the floor. "I apologize, Ember. I was only trying to be helpful. I was in a difficult position with you and your aunt…" She inhaled sharply. "Never mind. You're right. It was foolish of me."

I surprised myself by wrapping my arms around her and pulling her in for a tight hug. "I forgive you, Marigold. I know you only did it because you care about us, and that means more than you know."

Marigold sank against me. "I'm so relieved. I miss our lessons, Ember. I enjoyed taking you under my wing."

I released her. "I think you might owe Harold an apology, too. Just because he doesn't remember dating a raccoon or anything else during his time as a cat doesn't mean you can ignore what you did."

She sniffed. "Fair enough. I'm sure I can come up with a suitable apology gift."

"A gift card to a local restaurant might do the trick. I think he was pretty hungry in his cat form."

"Noted." She planted a kiss on my cheek and left.

I returned upstairs to shower and dress before Granger arrived for dinner. Marley was at Jinx's house for the night, so I only had to cook for two—and by cook, I meant order food to be delivered.

Florian texted to check on me and asked whether he was needed.

I'm good, thanks.

Phew. I have plans with Honey, but I would've cancelled.

No, you wouldn't have, but that's ok. I was glad he was moving forward with Honey. I had my fingers crossed for them.

I brushed my hair and examined the results in the mirror. I'd been eliminated from Natural Selection, obviously, but I resolved to make more of an effort with my appearance on a regular basis. I'd let myself go a little in the wake of my personal problems. According to Florian,

Sheridan had chosen Daisy, of course, and no one else discovered their plan.

"Miss Ember," a voice called.

"Simon, is that you?" I fled the bathroom and arrived at the bottom of the staircase to find Aunt Hyacinth standing alone in the middle of the living room. She wore a long cloak over her coral-colored kaftan. Her white-blond hair was loose today, a departure from her usual style. The front door clicked closed. Simon had beat a hasty retreat. Wise butler.

"It's good to see you upright," my aunt said.

My mind went straight back to the two of us on the kitchen floor. "How did you know I can do that kind of magic? The body swapping." I'd deliberately kept that ability a secret.

She wore a half smile. "Really, darling. Do you think the coven doesn't report to me? I may not be the High Priestess, but I am the one they look to for leadership."

And the one they feared.

"It was Marigold, wasn't it?" I didn't know why I bothered to ask. I knew it had to be. Marigold had experienced my Freaky Friday ability firsthand during one of our sessions in the woods. She must've told my aunt. I couldn't blame her. If I were in Marigold's shoes, I likely would have done the same.

"It doesn't matter. Now stop focusing on the negative. It's bad for your complexion." My aunt observed me from head to toe. "I must say, you're looking well. I wasn't certain what condition I'd find you in."

"I have you to thank for my recovery."

She offered a nod of acknowledgment. "You're family, Ember. We look after our own."

"Unless we disappoint you or disagree with you."

"In the past, there were certain conditions..."

I burst into laughter. "In the past? Try as recently as last week. Why were you even here? You rarely visit me."

She cleared her throat. "I came to apologize for my behavior. I've come to the conclusion that I have stagnated as a witch and as a leader of this coven and community. Much to my dismay, I have become an oppressor that only wields power for my own benefit, no matter how many committees I chair and how many nonprofits I run. I never intended that. In fact, as a young witch, I railed against such behavior. But we are doomed to repeat patterns we fail to break, aren't we?"

My mouth dropped open. I'd never heard such honesty from the ice queen. "What brought about this revelation?"

"I spent this past week at an exclusive magical retreat in a place called Two Rivers. A special place designed for contemplation and introspection."

"A glimpse into the void? How terrifying."

She sniffed. "As I said, I realized during my time there that I've been repeating a cycle. Treating you the way I was treated." She paused. "The way I loathed to be treated."

I nodded. "You and I could easily have been Evelyn and Sheridan Sinclair."

I expected her to scoff. Instead she said, "I do believe you're right."

Wow. You could've knocked me down with one of Marley's feather pens.

"Where do we go from here?"

She clasped her hands in front of her. "I'm glad you asked. I'd like to propose that we start over. Get to know each other as aunt and niece rather than as someone I feel the need to control and force into submission."

My heart swelled. "I like the sound of that." An idea

occurred to me. "This isn't a ploy to gain my trust and steal Ivy's magic when my defenses are down?"

Her expression crumpled. "I know it will take time to earn your trust and respect, but I'm willing to put in the effort. I regret that I was unable to repair my relationship with your father. I don't want to make the same mistake with you. The cycle ends right here, right now. I only want to be an aunt to you and Marley."

I could hardly believe my ears. "My father would be so happy to hear you say that."

"And what about you, Ember? I'm more interested in your thoughts."

Apparently I was on a hugging rampage, because I wrapped my arms around the shorter woman and squeezed. My throat was too dry to speak. This was the only response I felt capable of giving. She squeezed me back, understanding.

"We are powerful witches, Ember. We have a responsibility not only to the world, but to each other, to be the best versions of ourselves."

"I think we'd owe that to each other regardless of how powerful we are."

"Yes. You're quite right." She stepped back to examine me. "You should try standing a little straighter. Your posture..."

I arched an eyebrow.

"What? I didn't promise to never raise another valid criticism."

I sighed. "I guess I can't expect a complete one-eighty. More of a one-fifty."

"We are all a work in progress, are we not?"

I nodded. "Most definitely. Thank you for this. Marley will be so thrilled to be back at Sunday dinners."

"And I will be thrilled to set a place for you both." A shadow passed across her features. "About Alec..."

I waved her off. "Alec is responsible for his own actions."

"But those actions wouldn't have happened if not for my interference."

"I don't think that's true. Maybe I did at first, but he and I were having issues that had nothing to do with you. Getting fired from *Vox Populi* was just the nail in his coffin."

"I will no longer interfere in your relationships. Who you date is your business." She made a show of dusting off her hands.

"Just out of curiosity, are you making the same pledge to Florian and Linnea?"

She regarded me. "It seems only right, I suppose."

"If it's any consolation, I think Honey is thawing toward Florian. You might get your wish after all."

She allowed herself a tiny smile. "Isn't that the way of the universe? The moment I stop trying to make an appropriate connection for my son, it happens on its own. Lesson learned." She drew a breath. "Many lessons."

I escorted her to the front door, mainly because I needed to finish getting ready for Granger's visit. I didn't want to resemble a corpse bride when he arrived.

When I closed the door, Raoul was standing behind it. I clutched my chest. "Sweet baby Elvis! I didn't know you were here."

Sorry. I came in during the Big Speech and didn't want to interrupt such a magical moment.

"She might've turned you into a toad."

Or worse. A dog. He glanced at PP3. *No offense, my dude.*

The Yorkie didn't bother to raise his head from the throw pillow.

I'm sorry I wasn't there, he continued.

Magic & Marriage

"Sorry you missed out on the entertainment?"

No, I mean your near-death experience. I'm your familiar. I should've sensed your distress and come running.

"Maybe you didn't sense it because of the body swapping. It would've been confusing. Where were you?"

Getting over heartbreak, where else?

I rubbed his head. "I'm sorry."

I can choose to wallow or I can choose to learn a lesson. I'm choosing the lesson.

I peered at him. "And what is the lesson?"

To take my time. I rushed ahead without knowing enough about her.

"Everybody should get the chance to be a fool and rush in at least once in your life." I'd learned that lesson, too, and I'd never put myself in that position again.

Raoul looked at me. *You're not disappointed in me?*

I balked. "Disappointed? Why would you think that?"

I'm the brains of this operation. I'm expected to be above this sort of thing.

I resisted a smile. "Yes, the brains. I'm not disappointed, Raoul. I'm sorry this happened to you. I know how you feel." I leaned over and hugged him. "The right partner will come along. Just you wait."

His paws tapped my back. *If you're the only partner I ever have, it will be good enough for me. I'm your familiar first and a raccoon second.*

"Raoul, I never want you to feel you have to sacrifice an important part of yourself for my sake. That's not the kind of relationship I want us to have."

He released me. *I know. All I'm saying is that if it's you and me until the end of time, I could do worse. A lot worse.*

I touched his damp nose. "We do make a fine team."

PP3 growled in the direction of the door. Speaking of a fine team...

"Company," I said, and bounced to the front door. A solitary figure swaggered toward me, prompting an involuntary gasp from me. Granger Nash was decked out in a tuxedo. The waves of his dark hair had been meticulously tamed. In his hand, he carried a single red rose.

I opened the door and he brightened when he noticed me. "Nice to see you up and about."

"I heal quickly." I shrugged. "Rose blood. Are you on your way somewhere special in that outfit?"

"I'm already there."

I glanced at the rose but said nothing. I'd let him get there in his own time. "Come in. I haven't ordered yet, so if you have any suggestions, I'm all ears."

He crossed the threshold and I launched straight into the case. "I assume you found the tiny pricks in Tish's skin from the darts."

He nodded. "Just like your aunt said we would. How did you figure out it was her?"

"A few pieces of the puzzle fell into place at the right time."

He grinned. "The right time being right as she tried to kill you?"

I returned his good-natured smile. "Smart ass."

He extended the flower toward me. "For you. Consider it a balm on the wound I just caused."

"What? No giraffe?"

"A rose for a Rose seemed more appropriate."

I accepted the flower and immediately brought it to my nose for a sniff. "It's beautiful. Thank you. Is this how your office has decided to reward good citizens now? Solve enough crimes, get a bouquet?"

He grinned. "I'm not sure that'd be enough of an incentive for most folks to put their necks on the line in the name of law enforcement."

I twirled the stem between my fingers. "Then what's the occasion?"

Granger placed a hand against his chest. "You asked me why I'd never date Valentina Pitt and I didn't give you a straight answer, but only because I think the answer's obvious. She isn't you, Rose." He reached for my hand. "We've been through a lot together, the two of us. You made choices that hurt me deeply, but I understood them and respected them. So I decided to wait because, in my heart of hearts, I knew you'd come back to me someday."

He'd told me he would wait and, true to his word, he did. Gods above, there was nobody in the world like Granger Nash. Not a soul.

"Ember Rose, I'd like to officially request a second chance."

My throat thickened with emotion. "Shouldn't I be the one asking for a second chance? I'm the one who blew it the first time."

"Figured I'd save you the trouble. I know how stubborn you are."

I choked back tears. "You didn't have to get all dressed up to ask me. I would've said yes no matter what you're wearing."

He cocked an eyebrow. "Even my birthday suit?"

I smiled. "Especially your birthday suit."

He glanced down at his tux. "Now I feel like I've made a grave miscalculation."

I burst into laughter. "Any thoughts about dinner?"

Pizza, Raoul called from the safety of the kitchen.

Get out of here!

"Not really. What are you in the mood for?" Granger asked.

As hungry as I was, I couldn't wait another second. Using his bowtie, I pulled him toward me and planted a kiss on his lips.

"This."

* * *

Don't miss Magic & Midnight, the next book in the series!

To learn more about my books or to sign up for my VIP List and receive FREE bonus content,

visit www.annabelchase.com.

Printed in Great Britain
by Amazon